the
suspect

Georges Simenon

the
suspect

translated by Stuart Gilbert

A Helen and Kurt Wolff Book
Harcourt Brace Jovanovich, Publishers
New York   San Diego   London

HBJ

Copyright © 1991 by the Estate of Georges Simenon

All rights reserved. No part of this publication
may be reproduced or transmitted in any form or by any means,
electronic or mechanical, including photocopy, recording,
or any information storage and retrieval system,
without permission in writing from the publisher.

Requests for permission to make copies of any
part of the work should be mailed to:
Permissions Department,
Harcourt Brace Jovanovich, Publishers, 8th Floor,
Orlando, Florida 32887.

Published in the volume *On the Danger Line*
by Routledge in London, Copyright 1944 by Georges Simenon.
Copyright renewed 1972 by Harcourt Brace Jovanovich, Inc.
This is a translation of *Le Suspect*, Gallimard, 1938

Library of Congress Cataloging-in-Publication Data
Simenon, Georges, 1903–1989
[Suspect. English]
The suspect/Georges Simenon;
translated by Stuart Gilbert.—2nd ed.
p.   cm.
Translation of: Le suspect.
"A Helen and Kurt Wolff book."
I. Title.
PQ2637.I53S8513   1991
843'.912—dc20   90-26531
ISBN 0-15-137057-5

Designed by Lisa Peters
Printed in the United States of America
Second edition   A B C D E

the
suspect

1

THE STAGE DOORKEEPER must have been really angry, to yell like that. In spite of the distance separating them—it included a door, a flight of stairs, a long hallway—Chave, from the prompt corner in the wings, could hear every word he was shouting into the telephone.

"I tell you he can't possibly come now. He's on the stage."

It had been going on like this since the curtain rose for the first act: every few minutes the telephone had rung, and the doorkeeper had given the same reply, in tones of rising exasperation. The man had an obvious remedy, Chave reflected: he had only to leave the receiver off if he felt like that about it.

Chave drew back a little; he had just realized that he'd leaned too far forward, and a man in the front row was watching him with amused interest. Though by force of habit he kept an eye on the text as it was being played out on the

1

stage, he was thinking of a host of things at the same time. It was as if he had half a dozen independent brains.

For one thing, he was wondering whether it would turn out to be measles. His wife had called him at five, after the doctor had gone. The doorkeeper had made himself obnoxious, as usual, about the call, because, though the show hadn't begun, they were in the thick of rehearsal. The doctor, he gathered, had refused to commit himself; he wouldn't be able to say definitely what it was for a day or two.

Meanwhile, Pierrot was in bed with a high temperature, his cheeks flushed, and a quaintly indignant expression on his face, as if to reproach the grown-ups for their impotence. . . .

"You now!" Chave hissed to an actor in a policeman's uniform. The man's false mustache was held on with string that cut into his makeup.

The leading man shot him a furious glance from his place in the center of the stage, but Chave merely shrugged. Was it his fault he'd failed to dig up a bugle at the last moment for the "distant bugle call" prescribed in the stage directions? They couldn't expect him to be everything at once—prompter, producer, property man—and to play third man-about-town in the nightclub scene into the bargain.

He hadn't eaten. He'd only just found time to get into a gray morning coat—the only "dressy" garment he could lay hands on—for his entrance in the nightclub scene of Act Two. The leading man, an actor from Paris who thought he was a great star, had eyed it with disdain.

"So you wear morning coats in Brussels when you go to a cabaret?"

What did it matter anyway? The Parisian had been yelling himself hoarse since two in the afternoon, finding fault with everything, cursing the other actors, yelling for the

2

bugle that couldn't be procured. The result was that when the curtain went up he was almost voiceless. Actually, he had felt prepared for almost anything to happen, except for the stage to be ready in time for the performance, and for the local talent appearing with him to come in on cue.

Never had it poured in Brussels as it did that afternoon. At times the rain was like drumrolls on the glass roof of the theater. The checkroom attendants had put the streaming umbrellas in the hallways to drip, and an unpleasant odor of muddy shoes and soaked garments was coming from the public in the orchestra seats.

"Only twelve hundred francs in front," the Parisian actor had wailed, after he visited the box office shortly before the curtain rose. "And I'm on a percentage! They told me the house would be worth ten or fifteen thousand. Where's the manager?"

As usual on such occasions, the manager was nowhere to be found.

"I never saw such scenery! A miserable old drawing-room set for a fashionable nightclub! A glad-and-sorry dining-room suite for a baronial hall! And nobody knows his words. It's just too dreadful."

He had got on everybody's nerves to such a point that there had been talk about not going on, making an announcement to the public, and calling in an arbitrator. Indeed, it was almost a miracle that the performance was taking place, an audience in the house, the footlights on. Also that Pierre Chave was at his post, listening to the doorkeeper yelling for the nth time: "I tell you he can't come. He's 'on.'"

"Curtain!" hissed Chave to the electrician standing by, who didn't realize the act had ended.

On the stage, the man from Paris was rolling frantic eyes

3

at the curtain, which persisted in not falling. This didn't prevent his recovering his habitual smile for taking his bow, and as promptly removing it when he rushed up to Chave.

"What did I tell you? The whole of the first act's been ruined because there wasn't a bugle call in the big scene. I knew it would be like that. You can't say I didn't warn you. . . ."

From below, the doorkeeper was calling:

"Monsieur Chave! You're wanted, Monsieur Chave."

"Where are you off to?" the actor asked.

"Oh, I'll be back in a minute. There's someone to see me at the stage door."

"He can wait. I'm not finished with you yet. Who's that horrible old hag in purple I saw just now in the wings?"

"The Countess in Act Two."

"But, good God, you promised me . . ."

Chave brushed his way past the man and, script in hand, started down the iron steps, which were smeared with the traces of muddy boots. He had been in the theater without a break since nine in the morning, and he felt almost light-headed from hunger and fatigue.

He was far too exhausted to wonder who had been calling him up so persistently during the last half hour. If he had any idea in his head, it was of dashing across to the café opposite the theater for a snack and a glass of beer.

At the foot of the dimly lit staircase was a sort of vestibule, drafty and unswept, with doors on three sides. It was here that actors looking for a job were made to wait—and also theatrical suppliers wanting to be paid, and sometimes agents.

When Chave reached the foot of the stairs, a look of anger came into his eyes. He had just noticed a man in a heavy light-brown overcoat, with a briefcase in his hand, standing in the doorway watching him.

"Why the devil have you come here?" he asked irritably. He had forgotten that he was wearing a gray morning coat and that under the layer of greasepaint his face was expressionless as a waxwork figure's.

The man glanced around apprehensively and put a finger to his lips.

"I must have a word with you—in private."

The manager's office, on the right, was locked; so was that of the stage director, and the doorkeeper was in his cubbyhole at the entrance.

"Well let's go across the way." Chave was still thinking of his glass of beer.

"I wonder . . ." The man paused.

"What?"

"Oh, nothing. But one can't be too careful. . . . All right then, if you think it's safe."

He was obviously on edge, but, as Chave knew, that was his way; the least thing was enough to fluster him. A florid, corpulent man in his early forties, he always gave the impression of being in a tearing hurry. He gesticulated, gasped and spluttered, as he poured into his hearer's ears interminable stories of fantastic plots afoot, incredible adventures, and responsibilities graver than those of a premier in wartime.

His name was Baron, plain Monsieur Baron. Though he had no claim to noble rank, most of the people he associated with in Paris referred to him as "the Baron," and—at a distance—he sometimes looked the part.

Chave led the way across the street into the little café, where they were used to seeing actors drop in at all hours, often in their stage costumes. He promptly ordered a tankard

5

of beer and a sandwich, then held his hands toward the big stove, which was purring like a contented cat.

"When did you get here?" he asked.

"An hour ago. I went to the Veltam brasserie as usual, and called the theater."

"Yes. I heard. . . ."

"Did they give you my message?"

"No. I just heard the telephone ringing."

"That's why I came here. I had a hunch they wouldn't give you the message."

"Here's luck! Have one with me?"

"No, thanks. I've had all I want." The Baron scowled at the proprietor standing behind the bar, who was listening, unabashed, to the conversation. "Look! I have to talk with you—privately. You understand?"

"Meet me at the stage door after the show. We end early tonight."

"That might be too late. I'd rather tell you now."

With his pink cheeks, camel-hair coat, and briefcase bulging with papers, he might have passed at first glance for one of those jovial salesmen who transact their business over copious meals or in bistros. On closer look, however, it could be seen that his shirt was frayed and the showy overcoat worn at the cuffs and buttonholes.

"All right. Come back to the theater with me. We'll find a quiet corner somewhere."

"Your dressing room?"

Chave grinned. Was it likely he'd have a dressing room?

When they reached the foot of the iron stairs, he paused and, after a moment's thought, remarked:

"We'd better stay here. It's as good as anywhere else."

Still feeling tired, he lowered himself to a step, the driest he could see, and the Baron, reluctant though he was to soil

6

his coat, followed suit, turning up his collar against the draft.

"I can't help wondering if I've been trailed from Paris," he began nervously.

"Ah? Did you notice anyone?"

"No, I wouldn't say that. But in the train, you know . . . Still, I don't see how they could possibly have found out so soon. Well, I suppose I'd better tell you. . . ."

But he seemed reluctant to launch into his story, and kept glancing toward the doorkeeper's room, as if he suspected the man was listening. There was a rumbling overhead: sets being dragged across the stage.

"They've all gone quite crazy. Or K. has. He's got the whip hand and is egging them on. Yesterday I was told that young Rob had been . . . given a job to do."

Chave's face was inscrutable under the mask of makeup.

"What sort of job?"

The Baron hesitated, almost as if he felt responsible for the enormity of the thing he had to say. Then he announced, in a dramatic whisper:

"They've voted for direct action."

More and more impatient, Chave burst out:

"Damn it all. Don't beat around the bush! What sort of action?"

"I wasn't at the meeting. It was the Printer who told me. He said that Rob had been delegated to blow up a . . ." He paused again.

Chave got up.

"A . . . what? Have you lost your voice?"

"A factory. At Courbevoie, he said. An airplane-parts factory, I gathered, but he wasn't quite sure. It's for this week. That's all I know."

"And they want that poor kid Rob to do it?"

"Yes."

"Have you seen him?"

"No. I think they've told him to lie low till the time comes."

Chave gave a start. The grotesque-looking woman in mauve who was playing the Countess in the next act had suddenly appeared beside him, from nowhere it seemed.

"Well, what is it?" he snapped.

"I've been sent to get you. Something's wrong with the phonograph, and they want you to do something."

He shot her an almost murderous glance, then said to the Baron:

"Wait for me here. . . . No. Go to the Veltam. I'll meet you there."

He ran up the steps, three at a time, and burst into a dressing room, where three men were putting on their makeup. A heavy smell from the w.c. hung in the air.

"What is it?"

"I've got to leave at once. If anyone asks for me . . ."

"But . . ."

"Oh, go to hell!"

He had only his coat to change and the greasepaint to remove. On his way down the stairs again, he encountered the actor from Paris, who tried to stop him, but was too stupefied by his precipitate exit to get a word out.

The Veltam was a comfortable, well-kept brasserie with a homey atmosphere. The tables were always scrupulously clean, the waiters polite, and the beer mugs more generously filled than elsewhere. Chave found the man from Paris seated in a corner. He was fidgeting, and there was something like panic in his eyes.

"So you managed to get away?"

"A glass of ale, Jules. Yes, the 'extra-special.' . . . I didn't ask; I simply left. Do you have any money on you?"

8

"Two hundred and fifty francs or so."

"Hand it over."

"I'm sorry, but . . ."

"Hand it over, you fool. You can keep enough for your hotel. . . . Thanks. Now you'd better go and tell my wife. . . . No. She'll be in bed, or getting ready for it. Go tomorrow morning. But don't give anything away. Tell her I've gone on a trip to . . . Amsterdam."

"What are you going to do?"

"Can't you guess? I'm taking the next train to Paris. . . . Waiter, do you have a timetable?"

He had removed his makeup hastily, and the dusky rings around his eyes were more pronounced than usual. He was seething with excitement, and now and then, with an impatient movement, like a nervous tic, would toss his long dark hair back from his forehead.

"Good. There's a train for Mons in twenty minutes."

"What about the border?"

"I can take care of that. There's a bicycle under the stairs at the theater. I'll go back and get it."

"Shall I come with you?"

"No; stay here. Don't forget to go and see my wife. Remember the address?"

"Rue Snieder, isn't it?"

"Yes. Number 23 . . . Hell! I was about to forget the money."

He nearly forgot his raincoat as well. Once he was in the side street leading to the stage door, he broke into a run. Hearing a noise, the doorkeeper poked his head out.

"Oh, it's you at last. They've been . . ."

"Good night."

There was not a minute to lose. Jumping on the bicycle, he pedaled furiously to the station, slammed the bicycle into

9

the baggage car, and scrambled into a third-class coach just as the train was drawing out. His coat was dripping. For some time he remained standing in the corridor, watching the raindrops zigzagging down the window.

Rue Snieder, in the Brussels suburb of Schaerbeek, was silent and deserted. Two streetlights glowed through the rain-swept darkness, dimly lighting rows of small new houses and smoothly laid sidewalks.

Toward eleven there was a sound of footsteps; the door of Number 17 opened and was closed. Then all was silence again. At night there was never any traffic in the street, and the only sounds came from a railway line nearby. Sometimes a train whistled for a quarter of an hour or so, when shunting or held up by a signal.

Marie Chave was ironing in the kitchen. She was think-ing in the desultory way one thinks when ironing, and the slow sweep of the iron set the rhythm for her thoughts. Now and then she paused, took another iron from the stove, and, as she held it near her cheek to test the heat, listened to the breathing of the small boy sleeping in his tiny bedroom.

She knew that if she stayed up working too late it would mean more trouble with the owners of the house, who oc-cupied the ground floor. They were an old couple, the man a bank employee of thirty years' standing, the woman can-tankerous and a stickler for propriety, who disapproved on principle of late hours. The Chaves lived on the second floor, and all their movements could be heard below.

The bank clerk and his wife had never been able to rec-oncile themselves to the small inconveniences that inevitably occur when a house built for a single family is split up into apartments.

Though the rooms occupied by the Chaves were pleasant enough—new, well lighted, and reasonably large, except for Pierrot's—Marie would often sigh and say to her husband:

"Of course we might have done much worse, but somehow I never feel at home here."

One source of friction between the two households was the doorbell. Though there was a sign, in large letters—FOR CHAVE, RING TWICE—people were always making mistakes, and the old woman could be heard shouting angrily up the stairs:

"Someone else for you, Madame Chave!"

She was furious if the visitors failed to clean their shoes on the scraper outside the door. Another of her grievances was Pierre Chave's habit of coming home from the theater at one in the morning.

The patter of the rain was company in a way and, with the low murmur of the stove, the sound of Pierrot's breathing, and the warmth of the irons, helped to create an atmosphere of snug, self-contained domesticity. Even the alarm clock contributed to this; it had a distinctive tick, not in the least like that of other clocks—as if it, too, were regulated to the tempo of the household.

By the time its hands pointed to ten of twelve, Marie was beginning to feel an ache in her back, but she continued ironing, though more slowly, as if reflecting that she might as well go on until Pierre returned, if she had the energy.

When it was midnight, however, she put everything back in its place, methodically, went to the front door to make sure she had removed the key from the inside—otherwise Pierre couldn't put his in—and began undressing.

There was only a night-light in the child's room. Pierrot opened his eyes and looked up at his mother when she came in, but said nothing. This worried her, because usually it was almost impossible to make him hold his tongue.

"What do you want, Pierrot?"

"Thirsty," he whispered through parched lips.

She gave him a glass of water, holding her arm around his shoulders as he drank. Then she tucked in the sheets.

"Do you feel any pain?"

He merely sighed and shut his eyes, pouting a little.

Marie went to bed. She had left the light on the landing turned on, and a faint glow outlined the bedroom door. Now and again she heard the rumble of a train, but it didn't drown the steady tick of the alarm clock in the kitchen. Suddenly she reached out, lit a match, and glanced at her watch beside the bed.

It was one-thirty, and Pierre wasn't back yet! Well, she consoled herself, this wasn't the first time. As a rule he caught the last streetcar and got off at the Place Emile-Zola. But occasionally he was kept late, especially on opening nights. Sometimes, when rehearsals had gone on all day, and there had been no time to eat before the show, the company went in a body to a late-night bistro on Rue des Bouchers, and Pierre bicycled home. Once, he had had to walk home, because the messenger boy's bicycle wasn't available.

After a moment Marie got out of bed. She thought she smelled something burning, and went to the kitchen to check. But it was only the smell of ironing lingering in the air.

She went back to bed again and, after tossing for half an hour or so, managed to get to sleep, one arm resting on Pierre's empty pillow.

There was no possibility of steering around the puddles. There were too many, and, anyhow, the rain was coming down in torrents. Chave felt cold water pouring down his neck and along his spine. His trousers were stuck fast to his knees; spatters of mud stung his cheeks.

So much the better, for in weather like this it was unlikely that the Customs officers would be too alert. He had already covered eight miles from Mons: first on the main road, where there were still some cars, even though it was so late; after that on country lanes, where he was not so sure of his bearings. One of them had petered out in the yard of a factory with long lines of windows glowing red across the downpour.

There was a curious incongruity about this frontier region through which he was moving. Hardly had he passed a group of blast furnaces belching flames into the darkness when the air became redolent of cows and dunghills, the road was flanked by small farmhouses and cottages, and dogs started barking at him and rattling their chains.

He came to a series of small bridges, whether across the same stream or different ones he couldn't tell. Once, he heard voices behind a wall, unseen people quietly discussing their private concerns in the darkness. Customs officers, most probably; nobody else was likely to be out at this hour in such weather.

For some time he suspected that he was going in a circle. He hadn't the vaguest notion where he was or what the time was. Suddenly he saw a newly built steeple looming up ahead, and he recognized it as the Havay church.

This meant that the border lay only three hundred yards away, beyond the next bend. He jumped off the bicycle and wheeled it across a field, plowing his way through heavy mud and stumbling over mounds of sugar-beet refuse.

Soon he saw a light in front of him and, not knowing whether it was the Belgian or the French customshouse, he decided to give it a wide berth.

13

Once back on the road, he crouched over the handlebars and pedaled frantically. A sudden fear of missing his train had seized him. To his surprise, he found himself entering Maubeuge only a few minutes later. When he got off in front of the station, he found that the night train from Berlin to Paris, due in at one, was, as usual, late, having been delayed at the border.

The train was packed, and everyone asleep. Finally he managed to squeeze in between two women. Someone had had his feet on the place where he was sitting, and he could feel moisture oozing through the seat of his trousers.

He nearly went all the way to Paris, where the train was due to arrive at 7:30. Perhaps if he had been more comfortable, he would have given way to his fatigue. But he was famished—or his stomach was upset; he couldn't say which—and he got out at Compiègne.

There was a glimmer in the east, and the rain was not so heavy as at Brussels, no more than a drizzle, under which streets and roofs glistened in the gray light of daybreak. As he stepped out of the station, he noticed a small café and walked across to it.

Quite a long time, five years or more, had passed since Chave last set eyes on a counter of the kind inside, sheathed in beer-splashed zinc, or breathed the characteristic atmosphere of a French bar, in which the aromatic steam from a big coffee urn mingles with the fumes of beer and wine.

"Do you have any rolls?"

"The baker will be here in a few minutes."

Why, at Schaerbeek, did his wife wake with a start at six this morning, though ordinarily she never got up before seven? Perhaps in her sleep she had suddenly grown con-

14

scious of the empty place beside her. There seemed no point in trying to sleep again, and she went to the kitchen, where, after pouring a little kerosene on the kindling, she lighted the fire.

It was impossible to tell if Pierrot's temperature had fallen. He was very flushed, and his breathing was labored—but he was often like that in the morning.

She tried to console herself with the thought that her husband might have considered it wiser to spend the night in the city rather than come home in that deluge of rain.

At seven, she dressed, though it cost her an effort, and a little later Pierrot woke. He was in a fretful mood and whimpered when she spoke to him.

Then, when she went downstairs to get the milk and bread, which had just been delivered, she ran into the bank clerk's wife in the hallway. The two women exchanged frigid good-mornings.

The sky was paling with dawn, and the cold was keener. A coalman trundled his cart down the street, his head covered by an empty sack.

"I'm hungry, Mama," Pierrot wailed, but the doctor had warned her not to give him anything to eat before his next visit.

This took place at eight, at the beginning of his rounds. He left his galoshes on the landing. Marie was quite alarmed by his worried air after taking the child's temperature and his failure to make the usual comforting remarks.

As a matter of fact, it wasn't Pierrot he was anxious about, but his wife; she had had a severe heart attack during the night.

"I'll call again this evening," he said. "The symptoms aren't clear enough yet for me to give a positive opinion."

He was washing his hands, and now Marie realized that his thoughts were elsewhere. Just then there were two rings at the door. Her heart missed a beat.

"Excuse me, doctor," she said and hurried to the landing.

It was most unusual to have visitors so early in the morning, and she was afraid it meant bad news. Had Pierre had an accident?

To her surprise, she saw that the old woman downstairs, who normally ignored a double ring, had already opened the door. A genial voice hailed her from the hall below.

"Don't bother to come down, Madame Chave."

She recognized the Baron, but the sight of him gave her no comfort. His briefcase under his arm, a forced smile on his lips, he tramped heavily up the stairs.

"Sorry to trouble you at such an unearthly hour, but Pierre asked me to come see you first thing this morning and tell you there's nothing to worry about."

The narrow stairway seemed quite crowded, what with the doctor going down, the Baron flattening himself against the wall, and Marie standing on the top step. The old woman could still be seen, too, hovering below and trying to hear what was being said.

"Good-by then," said the doctor, "till this evening. If he seems really hungry, you can give him a little milk."

"Thank you, doctor."

Though Chave, to earn his living, had joined the theatrical profession, it was the Baron who in ordinary life looked much more like an actor. He had a naturally expansive manner and made the most of it, affecting a Falstaffian geniality, and playing to the gallery in and out of season. Now, for instance, he went up to Pierrot's bed and rumbled:

"Well, well, what's wrong with our little man? A nasty pain in his tummy?"

16

The child gave him a disdainful look. Meanwhile, the Baron was making elaborate motions to convey to Marie that he wanted to talk to her alone.

"I saw Pierre last night," he began eagerly, as they entered the dining room, "and he gave me a message."

"What's happened to him?" she asked impatiently.

He put on an air of mystery, even opening the door and looking out to make sure nobody was eavesdropping.

"Nothing's happened to him. You have no need to be alarmed. He's been sent on an important—I should say *highly* important—mission, and he's left at short notice for . . . let's say, Amsterdam."

"Why 'let's say'?"

"Because where he is is nobody's business, neither yours nor mine. Do you understand?"

"I prefer not to," she retorted angrily. "And I'd like to hear what's behind all this nonsense."

"Come, come, madame. You know quite well that Pierre is . . ."

"I know nothing at all, except that I've been terribly worried all night, and will go on being worried till he comes back."

"I'm sorry you take it like that. But it was absolutely necessary . . ."

"For you to come here and start him off on this precious 'mission' of yours? Why can't you do your own dirty work, instead of dragging Pierre into it?"

She was too upset to be polite, and, in any case, she had always disliked the Baron, and not only the Baron, but also most of the other men who came from Paris for mysterious conferences with her husband.

"And of course you *would* come for him just when his son is ill!"

17

"I assure you, madame . . ."

"When will he be back?"

"Much as I should like to tell you, I'm afraid I simply can't say."

"In other words, you've no idea when he'll be back."

She was feeling limp, inert. Perhaps the weather had something to do with it. Grumpily, she added: "Would you like a cup of coffee?"

"Well, if it wouldn't be too much trouble . . ."

She was wearing felt slippers, which made her seem shorter than usual. In the mornings she always had a washed-out look, and her cheeks had the pallor that comes from living too much indoors. Actually, she was robust and rarely ill. While pouring boiling water into the coffeepot, she asked:

"What's this latest tomfoolery you've been plotting, you and your 'group,' or whatever you call it?"

"You know quite well that I dare not breathe a word of it, even to you. And if Pierre was here, he'd say the same thing."

"Thirsty!" the small boy wailed from the next room, but, because the door was shut, his mother didn't hear him.

"Let me tell you this!" she almost shouted at the embarrassed Baron. "If I had my way, Pierre would tell the whole bunch of you to go to the devil. When a man's married and has a son, he has no business getting mixed up in such things."

As she spoke, the door opened, and Pierrot appeared, barefoot.

"Go back to bed—at once," his mother ordered.

"I'm thirsty."

"Go back to bed, I said. The milk hasn't boiled yet."

"Don't want milk."

18

"Didn't you hear what I said? Go back immediately. You'll only catch cold, and I don't want you here anyway."

There are days like this, when one's nerves are stretched—and of course everything conspires to make them worse. While she was pouring the Baron's coffee, the milk boiled over into the fire.

"Well anyway, he's not gone to France, has he?"

"I swear to you . . ."

"Swearing won't help. I know what a liar you are. But try to tell the truth for once."

"Well, I . . . I'm afraid I can't say where he's gone."

"I see. He *has* gone to France. And you let him go, though you know quite well the risk he'll run: that he's liable to be arrested the moment he crosses the border!"

"Do please let me explain. . . ."

Something prompted her to walk to the window and look out through the muslin curtain. Two men were standing on the other side of the street, looking toward the house. She swung around to the Baron.

"Didn't you come by yourself?"

"Of course I did. Why do you ask?"

"Come and look."

At that moment the two men walked across the street, and immediately there were two peals of the doorbell.

"But it's impossible!" the Baron groaned, his eyes big with disbelief.

"What's impossible?"

"That the police . . ."

"Impossible or not, they're here. And, since it's all your fault, I'll ask *you* to deal with them. I never heard of such a thing, coming to see people when you have the police on your track!"

When in a good humor, she looked no more than twenty.

But when, as now, she was angry, she looked double that age, and all her prettiness vanished.

The old woman was yelling up the stairs:

"Can't you hear? That ring was for you."

"I'm coming."

She felt like weeping—with rage and dismay. Still, as she passed a mirror, she paused for a moment to settle her hair and take off her checked apron, which she tossed into a cupboard.

As she stepped out to the landing, she said to the Baron over her shoulder:

"Now don't talk silly and make things worse."

2

UNDER NORMAL CONDITIONS, he looked his part: a jovial, easygoing man, the picture of good health. But in the morning, on an empty stomach, he gave a very different impression; it was as if he had been deflated during the night; his cheeks sagged, and he had the flabby shapelessness of a leaking rubber doll.

And occasions like the present always found him at his lowest ebb. He had been through too many such experiences, all unpleasant. Even as a youngster he'd learned to dread the police.

Of the two men who entered the apartment, he had seen one already: a burly, red-haired Belgian inspector, who seemed to have a predilection for silver pens and pencils; an array of them again protruded from his breast pocket. There was a twinkle in his eye, as though he were saying:

"I thought it wouldn't be long before we met again!"

The Baron was in an agony of apprehension that he might

say it out loud. For he was feeling guilty and remorseful, and it would be almost more than he could bear to hear from another's lips the taunts he was already leveling at himself.

"Madame Chave?" said the other inspector, without removing his hat.

"What do you want?"

"Where's your husband?"

"He's not in just now."

Brushing her aside, the man made his way into the dining room, then into the bedroom.

"But she told you he wasn't here," the Baron ventured to protest; so feebly, however, that he wished he'd held his tongue.

It was all his fault, as usual! From his earliest days, he had had the unhappy knack of saying and doing the wrong thing, of putting his foot in his mouth on every possible occasion. Yet it wasn't through obtuseness; he knew very well what he was doing. It was a sort of mental kink: the more precarious his position, the more he involved himself in a tangle of absurd and unconvincing lies.

This fantastic expedition to Brussels was a case in point. Yesterday he had visited a member of their group known as "the Printer" in the weird ramshackle building on Montmartre where he lived. The Printer had hinted darkly of the plot that was being hatched.

"Above all," he'd said, "we must make sure that Chave doesn't get wind of it. He doesn't hold with this sort of thing. And there's no knowing what he'd do if he knew. He might even inform on us."

The Baron had pledged not to breathe a word of it to anyone, not even to Lili. As always, it seemed, he hadn't a penny in his pocket, but before a quarter of an hour had passed he'd thought up a pathetic story about a poor woman who was going to have a baby, and the Printer had handed over all he had handy, about four hundred francs.

Enough to pay for a trip to Brussels several times over! And the cream of the jest was that, thanks to the Printer, who'd specifically told him not to do so, he was able to let Chave know. This sort of thing was nothing new; he'd been behaving this way all his life, egged on by some demon of perversity to double-cross his best friends, and when, as often happened, he was found out, becoming tearful.

And last evening, he'd acted in much the same way with Chave. When asked how much money he had, he'd lied, and kept back a hundred francs. Quite deliberately, of course. Earlier, in the train, he had been gloating over the prospect of a visit to that agreeable little bar behind the Place de Brouckère, to which he had hastened the moment he left his friend.

He'd had his briefcase under his arm, and in his heavy coat, at which one needed to look closely to see the signs of wear and tear, he looked like a prosperous businessman. That was what he liked; and he also liked the atmosphere of the small bar.

The two plump barmaids came and sat with him.

"You're from Paris, aren't you?" one of them remarked.

He beamed on them, pawed their ample curves, and told them stories that sent them into shrieks of laughter.

There was only one girl beside him after another customer came in.

"How about moving upstairs, my dear?"

"Nothing doing till we close."

So he had waited until closing time, drinking glass after glass of beer. He preferred not to recall certain details, now that he thought of them in the bleak light of the morning after. For example, when he'd told the girl:

23

"If you knew who I am and why I've come to Brussels, it would make you sit up, all right. Wait a few days, and it's likely you'll see something in the papers."

"Good God! You're a burglar, ain't you? . . . Or a broker off on a spree with his clients' money? We've had some of that sort here."

He had smiled in a superior manner, to convey to the girl that such banal misdemeanors were beneath him. . . .

No, it was better not to think about all that. It was too embarrassing. The bar was really the lobby of a small hotel that was half brothel, and he'd had to wait till three in the morning to go up to his room, where the girl had joined him a quarter of an hour later.

Why had he acted like that? How often he had asked himself that question! The only answer he could find was that, worse luck, he couldn't help himself.

The girl had proved, as so often, a disappointment. She had haggled over the price and brushed aside his ponderous caresses as if they bored her.

"Hurry up!"

"Don't you sleep here?"

"I sleep upstairs—in the attic, if you must know."

Ten minutes after she had left him, when he was just dropping off to sleep, there was a peremptory knock on his door.

"Police! . . . Your passport, please."

Had the girl reported him? Or were the police merely doing a routine inspection of the less reputable hotels? Idle speculations; now that they'd come, there was nothing to do but face up to it.

The red-haired inspector had checked his papers. He had a notebook with him, presumably a list of suspects and persons "wanted," which he consulted now and then.

"When did you come to Brussels?"

"This evening."

"Whom have you met?"

"No one."

"Why have you come here?"

"On business."

This morning, he could guess what had happened. On checking him out, they had learned that he frequented anarchist circles. So they'd watched him, and shadowed him here. He hardly dared to meet Marie's eyes. From the way she was looking at him, he guessed that she suspected it was his blundering, if not worse, that was the cause of this upset in her domestic life.

"Now, madame," the inspector said, "will you tell me when your husband left?"

"I couldn't say. It must have been quite early."

Unlike the Baron, Chave's wife grew bolder in the face of danger. Seeing the inspector go down on his hands and knees to look under the bed, she remarked, ironically:

"That's right! Make yourself at home, and don't mind me!"

And she watched the police with a scornful eye while they ransacked the little apartment. Now and then she would go to her son, who was showing signs of alarm, and say soothingly:

"It's all right, Pierrot. There's nothing to worry about. Try to go to sleep. I'll bring you your milk when they've gone."

The Baron, who still had his coat on, was beginning to feel the heat as the police went about their work methodically, taking their time. Watching them, he wondered if they were acting on definite information, or did the fact that he, the Baron, had come to the house of a notorious anarchist, on whom the authorities had had their eyes for several years, account for this visit?

Probably, he decided, they had something definite to go on, for they were making a thorough job of it, opening closets and drawers, searching the pockets of an old suit of Chave's that was hanging in a wardrobe.

There were only three rooms—the dining room, bedroom, and kitchen—plus Pierrot's cubbyhole of a bedroom. The Chaves had their meals in the kitchen; so the dining room served as living room and, in particular, study. Chave did all his writing there, and the table was strewn with books and pamphlets.

It was a depressing room, like the common parlor in poor students' boardinghouses. The tablecloth was stained and tattered; signed photographs were fixed to the walls with thumbtacks; there was an imitation-marble mantelpiece, with a clock under a glass dome, and a small discolored dark ceramic stove.

"If you have work to do, madame," the inspector said, "you can get on with it, and leave us here. We'll be quite a while, I expect." And he coolly seated himself at Pierre's table, filled his pipe, and started studying the books and documents, one by one. The other inspector, a younger man, had just discovered the Baron's briefcase. He dumped it on the table in front of the red-haired inspector.

"We'll look through that later. Stand by the door and see that no one enters or leaves. You two," the older man added, turning to Marie and the Baron, "you'd better go to another room. I don't want you here."

He was behaving as if he owned the place: he'd drawn the ashtray within easy reach, and Marie suspected it was her husband's tobacco he was smoking.

26

"Isn't it time to give your boy his breakfast?"

She went to the kitchen, and the Baron slunk out after her, like a whipped dog. He hardly dared raise his eyes, and seemed embarrassed by his corpulence. For some minutes he lingered at the window, watching the rain falling on the empty street. The sky was such a neutral gray it could have been morning or nightfall. All the color seemed to have been washed out of the housefronts. At almost every window a nondescript green plant languished in a brass or copper pot. What could the people in those drab rooms be doing with themselves?

"Here!" He turned and saw Marie holding out to him, ungraciously, a steaming cup of coffee. The dining-room door was ajar, and he could see the policeman copying extracts from one of the pamphlets into his notebook.

After a moment's hesitation, Marie took a cup of coffee to him, too. Glancing up, he muttered a word of thanks, then went on with his work.

Every time she came near him, the Baron averted his eyes, though once he summoned up the courage to whisper: "There's nothing to be alarmed about."

But he was the last man to be capable of reassuring her. Had he told her frankly where Pierre was, it might have been different. However, she could guess. If he'd really been going to Amsterdam, he wouldn't have made all this mystery of it. She was convinced he'd gone to Paris—where, if caught, he was liable to a year's imprisonment, if not more.

"Now, Monsieur Baron, I'll have a little talk with you," the inspector said.

The briefcase lay open on the table, and the man had extracted from it two very unexpected objects, which explained why it had looked so bulky. They were model boats:

one of roughly carved wood, the other of cork hacked out with a penknife and embellished with loops of thread, pins, and wooden knobs.

"Well? What's the explanation of these things?"

"Oh, it's quite simple really," the Baron said uncomfortably. "Not at all what you imagine." He meant that these boats had nothing to do with espionage, or national security, or anything like that.

"You'll find the explanation in my briefcase," he added. "In that file with the blue cover . . . Yes, that's it. I'm working on an invention—an unsinkable lifeboat. I've taken out three patents already, and I'm hoping to sell them."

It was true, and the inspector guessed that at once. Without a smile, he aligned the two boats one behind the other, almost as if he were going to play with them.

"And is this the reason for your trip to Brussels?"

"Well, not altogether, but . . ."

"Then perhaps these are." He pointed to a sheaf of anarchist literature that filled one side of the briefcase.

"There's nothing wrong with those. You can buy them anywhere. They aren't even banned in Belgium."

Now and then Marie, who had started her housework, came and peeped into the room. After an hour or so, she began to get impatient.

"How much longer will you be?"

The air in the room was blue with smoke. The inspector had lighted the stove and kept it going full blast. Judging by his manner, he didn't seem to think that his investigation would come to much, but he was doing his job conscientiously. Perhaps, too, he was glad of a pretext for staying in a warm, cozy room, instead of going out into the pouring rain. There were moments when he seemed to find a certain pleasure in the spectacle of the big man's discomfiture—one could have sworn his fat was melting under the influence of fear—and in exasperating Madame Chave.

"I'd be through much quicker if you'd say where your husband is."

"I tell you, I don't know."

"Well, you can say whether or not he slept here last night."

"No, I can't!"

He turned to the Baron.

"What time did Chave leave?"

"How would I know?"

"Don't act the fool! What train did he take?"

"I assure you . . ."

From time to time Marie went to the small boy's bedside and bent over him. He didn't complain or show any signs of suffering, but his cheeks were still very flushed, his eyes fever-bright, and he was staring at the ceiling in a sort of waking dream.

"If you propose to stay much longer, I shall go out and do my marketing."

"Do so, by all means."

It was more exasperation than necessity that drove her outdoors. As she passed through the hallway, a door opened furtively and, seeing the old woman eying her malignantly, she felt like sticking her tongue out at her—or bursting into tears. But she did neither. Wrapping her shawl more tightly around her shoulders, purse in hand, she stepped out into the rain. There were three housewives waiting their turn to be served in the general store at the corner, and one of them asked Marie:

"Is it measles?"

29

"The doctor's not sure yet."

"I hope it isn't. It would be a dreadful nuisance if we had an epidemic of measles in the street."

Not to depart from her usual habits, she bought a chop, some vegetables, and the makings of a soup. On her return, she found the inspector still writing away, in a small neat hand. The Baron had drawn a chair to the bedside and was watching the sleeping child.

Everything was exactly the same as when she'd left, and this did not surprise her. Nevertheless, coming in from outside, she was struck by the strangeness of the scene. The light may have had something to do with it—an undersea greenish-gray light—and the curious smell in the air, of fever and burned milk. Or perhaps it was the sight of the red-haired inspector seated in Pierre's chair at Pierre's table, smoking a pipe that might have been her husband's. Oddest of all was the spectacle presented by the fat man at the bedside, whose humble, timid eyes seemed to plead for her forgiveness. And there were the two absurd little boats sitting on the table near the ink, and the other policeman, seated at the door, reading a newspaper.

After taking her purchases from her shopping net, she replaced her purse in the drawer of the kitchen table. Then she took out her handkerchief to blow her nose, and at last her tears began to flow—at the injustice of it all: that people like her, her husband, and her little son had to suffer such indignities.

She went on weeping silently as she cleaned the vegetables and put her soup on to boil. When, after half an hour, she saw the inspector rising from his chair, she had self-control enough not to ask anything, or seem to notice him.

"Take this gentleman to my office," he said to the man at the door, pointing to the Baron. "I'll be there presently."

He put on his coat and hat, picked up the briefcase, in which he had replaced the two small boats, and, after bowing to Marie, started down the stairs.

"Don't be alarmed," the Baron whispered to Marie as he, too, went out.

She preferred not to look at him. After a moment, she opened the door an inch and listened. She heard the inspector knocking at the door below, and he remained closeted with the old woman, Marie's bête noire, for nearly an hour.

Now that she was alone with her son, she had a curious feeling of being isolated from the world, as if she had been marooned with him in some strange remote place, from which there was no escape. The sight of the tranquil little street gave her no comfort; indeed, so alien and unfriendly did it seem that she drew back quickly from the window.

Yet she'd had plenty of time to get used to Belgium and its ways; it was about five years since they'd left Paris, and they had not set foot in France again. During all that time—because of Pierre, of course—her family had refused to have anything to do with her, and the only French people she met were of a curious type: would-be world shakers, gaunt and famished-looking men and women, who came to visit them now and again and had serious discussions with her husband in the study.

"Do you really think it's the best solution?" she had asked him one evening, when their visitors had left. The study reeked of cheap cigarettes, and empty glasses stood on shelves as well as the table.

"If everyone acted as I act . . ." he began.

"But everyone doesn't act as you do, Pierre—and never will!"

"Who can tell? Perhaps a day will come . . ."

There were moments when she wondered if Pierre himself wholly believed in the theories he enounced with such fervor; but she'd never dared to put a direct question to him on this. It might shake his faith; and if he lost faith, he'd lose half his interest in life. Yet, she *knew* . . . !

No, she hadn't the right to put ideas into his head. There are some things it doesn't do to admit, even to oneself. The Baron, for instance, couldn't admit to himself that he was a windbag, and a coward.

Pierre had had ten months' military service behind him when she left her parents' home in Paris to follow him to Bourges. Because he had only his army pay, she had gotten a job in a confectioner's. Then one fine day—fine in a manner of speaking, for it was raining hard and both of them were feeling low—he had noticed at last that she was pregnant.

By then, he had already begun to dally with those "advanced" ideas that were to make him a man apart. He read books that aren't found in ordinary bookstores and wrote articles that couldn't be printed. Still, he had performed his military duties conscientiously, and all might have gone well had he not fallen foul of his sergeant.

Even so, the situation might have been smoothed over if it hadn't been for *that*. . . . If it hadn't been for Pierrot, and the lack of any alternative, would they have crossed the border one night in the corridor of a third-class railway coach?

And would such a well-educated and clever man as Pierre have brought himself to apply for a job as extra at a small theater? And would he still be earning a precarious livelihood as assistant stage manager and prompter?

There had been a kind of fatality about it all, she concluded. But she had never breathed a word of her regrets to her husband. He read her the articles that he then sent to anarchist and left-wing papers. Some of his work had been printed clandestinely in Paris. And sometimes one of the strange men who came to the little apartment would say to Marie in an awed whisper:

"He's another Lenin!"

Once a woman, whose face was pitted from smallpox and who had taken part in some political violence in Paris—Pierre had found her a job at a brasserie in Brussels—had cried enthusiastically:

"He's a modern Savonarola!"

Pierrot was still awake. He was having trouble breathing, and his little mouth would open silently. Marie couldn't help thinking of a fish gasping its life out on a riverbank. What alarmed her most was his silence; it was so unlike him.

"Sure you haven't any pain?"

He merely shook his head, so slowly that each movement could be measured in seconds.

"What's wrong then?"

As if he felt obliged to make some answer, he murmured:

"Thirsty."

If he'd never come into the world, would Pierre . . . With an effort she brushed the thought aside and went for a glass of milk.

"Here you are."

A train was rattling past on the nearby line. From morning till night this sound could be heard, but it was only when you paid attention that it got on your nerves.

Pierrot drank his milk in little sips as he looked up at his mother with a half-reproachful expression that wrung her heart.

Less than a month before this, Chave had written to young Rob:

"Mind you tell me all you can find out about the newcomers, especially that fellow K., of whom I have my doubts. You, I know, can be trusted, whatever happens, and so can many of our group: in fact, the great majority. But bear in mind that not all of those who want to join us are led to do so because they really share our faith.

"Some of them are merely out for thrills or adventure. And there are traitors, too, and persons who act from secret and unworthy motives.

"I was not at all satisfied with the manner in which K. was introduced to the group; nor did I care for the tone of his last speech. I should have liked to meet him and judge for myself, but I gather that he refuses to come to Brussels.

"As soon as I can save a little cash I'll send it along, and you must come and spend a Sunday with us. I am sure you have a great many things to tell me, and I know that writing letters isn't easy for you. . . ."

He could ramble on like this page after page, like a man chatting with a lifelong friend, not troubling to choose his words. And while he wrote, he ceased to see the row of jerry-built houses outside his window, the dying plants in copper pots, the gray monotony of the suburban street. Instead, visions of a world of shining hope floated before his eyes.

He loved "little Rob" as he would have loved a brother younger than he was and more unfortunate. For Robert seemed predestined to misfortune, as some are born idiots or cripples. Chave knew all about his parentage—his Polish father and his French mother, a waitress in a cheap restaurant—since Robert had a habit of narrating the story of his life, in the tone of one reciting a poem or a set piece, and seemed to find gloomy pleasure in doing it.

His father suffered from a chronic disease that ran in the family. His mother had been delivered prematurely, and when Robert was a baby, she had tried to kill herself and him, in the manner of poor people: by sealing the kitchen door and windows and turning on the gas. She succeeded for herself, but somehow he survived.

Since then his life had been a series of mishaps and setbacks. For instance, when he was eleven, a charitable institution had found him a job on a farm, but no sooner was he getting used to the work than his father, just out of prison, turned up unexpectedly and insisted on taking him away. When he was thirteen, the police had caught him stealing from a market stall. And so it had gone on.

It was a mystery how he had learned to read and write, but once he had learned, reading and writing became his ruling passion. So much so that in order to keep in touch with printed matter he now was working as a bicycle messenger for one of the Paris daily papers.

"Your letter distressed me," he wrote in answer to Chave. "You are doing K. a grave injustice. Of course a pure-blooded Frenchman like you cannot understand him as I do, thanks to my Slav blood. But let me tell you . . ."

K., whom Chave had never met, was a Serbian. He had suddenly appeared at Paris, armed with letters of introduction from anarchist organizations in various parts of Europe.

"He is only thirty," Robert had continued, "but he has already put in some really great work for the Cause. I do wish you could meet him and, above all, hear him speak. Then I am sure you would come to share the high opinion of him that we all have. Of course I don't include such semibourgeois hangers-on as the Baron, who shakes like jelly every time he sets eyes on K."

The letters that passed between them on this topic read almost like a lovers' quarrel. Indeed, Chave couldn't disguise a touch of jealousy of K., to whom he attributed all the arts of seduction. Cruelest cut of all was that Robert, who hitherto had sworn by Chave and wholeheartedly accepted the Chavian outlook, was now a warm admirer of the Serb, and seemed to have swallowed all his theories wholesale.

"Don't forget that I am much older than you," Chave wrote, "and have—painfully enough—acquired a certain knowledge of the world. Here in Brussels, I keep my eyes open and can't help seeing that often our ideals are exploited by unprincipled adventurers, and suspecting that even dirtier work is going on behind the scenes. So it's up to me to warn you (I wouldn't say this to anyone else) against trusting blindly in a man like K."

Was he sincere, or merely jealous? Both at once, most probably. And he let himself be exasperated by such trivial details as the fact that recently the group had decided to shift their headquarters to a Paris suburb, Puteaux, and were now meeting in a place he had never seen. Before this, he had been able to visualize their meetings quite clearly, because he had often been to the barnlike room on the upper floor of an abandoned café where these took place. It was in a working-class district of Paris, and he could easily conjure up the atmosphere—squalor and enthusiasm—that prevailed at these gatherings; could hear the clang and clatter of the streetcars passing in the narrow street below. True, he'd been told that the streetcar tracks had been taken up; but that made no difference. For him, those fiery debates still took place to the rhythm of metal wheels. . . . Puteaux, however, meant little more than a name to him.

K., he was told, had introduced several new comrades, who, like himself, had traveled widely in Europe. "He considers our methods old-fashioned," Robert wrote, "and thinks our movement has lost its driving force."

A week earlier, one of Robert's letters had stung Chave into speaking his mind quite clearly:

36

"I trust I am wrong, but I am beginning to wonder if this Comrade K. you think so much of isn't simply a common agent provocateur, or, at best, an emissary of the Fourth International, which, of course, has no sympathy with our ideals. Don't forget what Trotsky said in his last message. . . ."

And now they were going to blow up a factory—to prove, presumably, that the movement hadn't "lost its driving force." Needless to say, it wasn't K., or any of his friends, who was assigned to plant the bomb. They had picked on Robert for the job—on "little Rob," whom Chave had shaped, and who during these last few weeks had been throwing off his influence.

Unfortunately, the Baron had been unable to say anything definite. He could give neither the date nor the hour appointed, nor even name the factory they intended to blow up.

Chave bicycled along the Seine as far as Puteaux, which he reached at lunchtime. He had swept his eyes over the factories and warehouses beside the river, one of which catastrophe was threatening, and, for the first time, fully realized the difficulties that lay ahead. There was no question of getting in touch with Robert, or the Printer, or any of his other friends; surely the police had them all under more or less constant observation.

In fact, during the last hour or so, he'd felt that he, too, was being followed, and as he rode back along the riverbank, he kept casting nervous glances over his shoulder. Each time a taxi or car overtook him, he had an uncomfortable feeling that its driver might have passed the word to someone in another vehicle behind, who then picked up the trail.

Beyond a bend of the Seine and a small green island with muddy banks, was the industrial suburb of Courbevoie. Before he reached it, the rain had stopped, but he was wet to the skin, despite his raincoat, and shivering from the cold, so he entered a small café and asked for a meal.

"My God! You look like a drowned rat!" the proprietor exclaimed as Chave lowered himself stiffly to a chair.

He was not merely soaked through, but also thoroughly exhausted; so much so that when his food was brought he could hardly eat. After a couple of glasses of red wine, he felt his eyes closing.

"Can I have a room?" He had noticed earlier that the upper portion of the place was a hotel.

"For tonight?"

"I'd like one right away, if you can manage it. I made a very early start."

"Ah, you've come a long way then?"

He had to be on his guard, so he gave a vague reply.

The proprietor led him up a flight of stairs to a small room with a very narrow window overlooking the river, and a red-tiled floor like those seen in farmhouses.

"Shall I take your things to dry while you're resting?"

Had he not been so tired he would have said "No." It was not wise to risk being stranded without clothes in a hotel bedroom, and thus be at the mercy of any emergency. But his one wish was to sleep; he couldn't be bothered with explanations.

About to drop off, he imagined he heard the voices of actors and felt the dust of a badly swept stage tickling his nostrils. He caught himself wondering if the Louis XVI chest needed for Act Three had been delivered in time.

Not only was there the red-tiled floor to give the illusion of being in the country, but the room had the characteristic odor of the French riverside inns he once knew so well: a complex smell of moldy cupboards, w.c.s, and fried fish.

He could hear a buzz of voices in the café below. As he rolled the immense eiderdown off the bed onto the tiles, a telephone rang. It made him wonder if it would be safe to call Robert at the newspaper office.

Was Pierrot better, or did he really have measles? The Baron must have gone first thing in the morning and told Marie some crazy story, which she certainly wouldn't believe. She was always like that; she never believed what people said. She was mistrust incarnate! Chave wondered sometimes if she believed what he, her husband, told her.

It was strange that, though he was back in his beloved France, he hardly realized it; he hadn't felt the faintest thrill. He had pedaled along thinking about what to do next, and eaten blindly, unconscious of his whereabouts.

Again the telephone rang. Had the proprietor's suspicions been aroused? Was he the kind of man to . . . ? No. He must stop thinking, and try to get some sleep. Rest was what he needed, and he let his mind blur and his limbs relax on the soft warmth of the mattress. He had a feeling of sinking swiftly through the void, as if he were in a well-oiled elevator. Yet he was still conscious of the country smell and seemed to hear, through veils of sleep, the buzzing of the telephone.

3

IT WAS FIVE in the morning when he woke, having slept without a break since the previous afternoon. Besides the now familiar smell, there were other details that struck pleasant chords of memory: the wardrobe, for instance, lined with flower-patterned paper, the narrow window almost at floor level—the room had probably formed part of a stable in earlier days—and the electric bulb, so weak a candle would have given better light.

He had no soap, razor, or toothbrush with him, so he merely ran a damp towel over his face. Finding his dried clothes outside the door, he got into them.

Though he trod as lightly as possible, some of the steps creaked as he went downstairs. In the café he found a girl in clogs, scrubbing the floor.

"Leaving?" she asked, more by way of making conversation than anything else.

"No. I happened to wake early, and I'm going for a walk."

"I wouldn't go out if I were you. It's still raining. Monsieur Georges will be down in a minute and he'll give you a cup of coffee."

"Good. I'll be back in a quarter of an hour."

He was depressed, or, rather, dissatisfied with himself, for not feeling the way he'd expected to. Not that he was unmoved, but such emotion as he felt was due less to the serious emergency that had brought him back to France than to trivial things, vague memories floating through his mind, sentimental associations with the past. This light drizzle falling through the gray morning, for instance, reminded him of his army days, the barracks yard echoing with the noise of horses under an autumn shower.

He gazed down at the sluggish river—more precisely, at an arm of the river, because the island lay immediately in front of him. Like everything that morning, it had a forlorn air. The slopes covered with weeds and tangled brushwood stirred some half-forgotten memory. . . .

Courbevoie, he knew, came after the next bridge, and he walked quickly in that direction. It had just occurred to him that he had better put some distance between himself and the café. If he paid for his room, he'd have almost no money left. The thought was galling, humiliating—but there was nothing else to be done.

Why did it take such an effort to put his mind on the job ahead of him? He had come to Paris with a definite purpose: to prevent a bomb from exploding and killing, likely as not, a number of people. But his thoughts seemed to be out of hand; he couldn't concentrate. He stopped and looked down at a big powered barge. The cabin was lighted, and he pictured the people inside dressing or drinking their morning

41

coffee. This brought back to his mind the café-hotel where he'd slept, and it struck him that he had left the bicycle there. He'd completely forgotten about it!

As so often when one gets up too early, he felt at a loose end. He foresaw that he would get soaked through again, but there was no help for it. The one bright spot was that he could be pretty certain he was not being shadowed. There was a clear stretch of nearly a mile of quayside between the Courbevoie and Neuilly bridges, and not a soul was in sight. He had the spectacle of the slow gray dawn to himself.

He ran his eyes over the buildings along the river. There were some small houses, but for the most part the river frontage was occupied by factories and big fenced-in yards, one of which held his attention for a moment. Through a chink between palings, he saw an enormous shed with canvas walls bellying like a ship's sails in the morning wind. A sign announced: TARPAULINS AND GROUNDSHEETS FOR RENT.

It struck him that if he had to go into hiding, this would be the ideal place. Rolled up in a groundsheet, in the shed, he would be under cover and safe from observation. He went to the gate and looked between the bars to make sure there was no watchdog.

Actually, he still had no clear plan for even the immediate future. He had left Brussels on a sudden impulse, horrified by the danger threatening heaven knew how many innocent people. Now that he was on the spot, he felt less sure of himself.

He passed another factory, a very large one, with a gate-keeper's lodge at the entrance, a big clock above the gate, and, above the clock, a bell. Then came heaps of bricks and tiles aligned beside the river, a few cranes, some barges moored side by side, and then a group of really imposing buildings: VICTOR ROCHE, AIRPLANE PARTS.

Hearing footsteps behind him, he looked around quickly. A bedraggled old woman had just crept out of the mound of sacks under which she had spent the night. Their eyes met, and though nothing was said by either, Chave couldn't shake off for quite a while the curious impression the encounter made.

The Courbevoie bridge lay only a hundred yards ahead, and the first trucks of the day were crossing it. Lights were on in the old tollhouse and in the two small cafés facing each other on the corners of the street leading to the bridge.

Chave had walked as slowly as he could, and there was only a short time before full day. Crossing the street, he entered one of the cafés. There was only one customer: a man loaded down with fishing tackle, talking over the bar to the proprietor.

"A coffee with a dash of cognac, please," Chave said.

After serving him, the proprietor continued his conversation with the fisherman.

"Well, what did he say?"

"He said that if things didn't improve, he was through with it."

"Did he? Well, that's how I feel, too."

What were they talking about? Though he stayed five minutes or so, Chave had to leave without knowing. He crossed the bridge, walking for walking's sake, and, looking back, saw the fisherman going down the bank to a place where evidently he was accustomed to stand, since he seemed to find his foothold on the slippery soil without having to look down. Probably, Chave surmised, he had steps already cut. And yet—could he be sure the man was really a fisherman?

Buses were passing, and people springing up from nowhere and hurrying along in all directions. After unlocking the iron gates, the gatekeeper of the airplane-parts factory took a big Alsatian dog for a run along the embankment.

The Baron had been distressingly vague; he really seemed to have no idea when the action was to take place or how they proposed to accomplish their plot. By now it was broad daylight, but Chave's eyes had grown used to the gradual increase of light and he was unaware that the sun had come out, weakly. One of the cranes had started up and was lowering tiles to the bank; two men, hooded with sacks, were stacking them in symmetrical heaps.

Needless to say, the idea of a bomb was not new to Chave. For years, at all their meetings and in conversation, the question of employing violent methods had been discussed, and he had heard endless disquisitions on the best recipes for high-explosive compounds, detonators, and so forth.

But it was a far cry from that academic, innocuous talk to the stark reality confronting him as he gazed at the slow, dark waters of the Seine, flecked with tiny silvery rings from the still-dripping trees, the fisherman standing motionless on a little pier of stones he had doubtless built himself, the barges, the swinging arm of the crane, the workers beginning to pour into the factory, the Alsatian dog returning from its run and lifting a leg at every pile of bricks. Unconsciously, he heard scraps of remarks exchanged by passersby, the squeal of bus brakes as they took the corner of the bridge, the tooting of a tug leaving the Suresnes lock.

"No!" he suddenly exclaimed aloud—as if the word were enough to settle everything.

He turned into a café and had another coffee. By the time he came out, there were five men fishing on the riverbank, with intervals of only a few yards between them.

On the way from Brussels, he had decided that the best way to deal with the situation would be to keep watch near

44

the factory and intercept young Rob when he came with his bomb.

It was one of those plans that sound feasible at a distance; but on the spot he realized it wouldn't be so simple. For one thing, he had discovered that there were two entrances to the factory: one used by the workmen; the other, in a back street parallel with the quay, used by the office staff. Very likely their plan was to blow up the offices; a small bomb would probably have more effect there. Obviously it was impossible for him to keep an eye on both entrances.

And this wasn't all. If he had to stay on watch for even two days, he was bound to be noticed. He had thought the proprietor of the café at the corner had eyed him intently, as if wondering who he could be. And the earliest of the fishermen had glanced up at him several times as he strolled back and forth on the riverbank.

It was all very well to affect a casual manner, to stop now and then to gaze idly at a barge, like a man who has nothing to do—but it wasn't convincing! Nobody in his right mind would loiter in a place like this, for the mere pleasure of the view, especially on such a damp morning.

Moreover, trucks were constantly being driven into the factory yard. What was there to prevent Robert from smuggling himself in on one of them?

The obvious course was to go to Montmartre, look up the Printer, and ask him to send for Robert. But that would be too risky. He knew that most of the group were on the police list of suspects and under more or less constant observation. And quite possibly the Baron had been followed all the way to Brussels and back. Therefore, there might well be a plainclothesman on the quay at this very moment, watching Chave.

He went to another café, one with a telephone, and, after

carefully closing the door of the booth, called the newspaper for which Robert worked.

"Can I have a word with one of your messengers?" he began.

"Sorry; it's against the rules," a girl's voice replied, and he guessed she was going to hang up.

"Listen, mademoiselle! It's terribly urgent. Surely you make an exception if . . . if, for instance, one of the boys' mothers is dying."

"All right. I'll put you through to the Sales Department," the girl replied in a bored tone.

"Sales? Can I speak to one of the messengers? Robert, his name is."

"Which Robert?"

"A little fellow. All skin and bones."

"Just a minute."

The silence that followed lasted so long he thought he'd been cut off. Meanwhile, he was twice disturbed by someone trying, rather forcefully, to the telephone. At last a voice spoke on the other end of the wire.

"Hello? Is it you who were asking for Robert? We haven't seen him here for two days."

"Can you give me his address?"

"No . . . What's that about his mother?"

"Nothing . . . Thank you."

He hung up and, as he stepped out of the booth, collided with the man who had been trying to get in. He noticed that he was given a hard stare.

"How much is that?" he asked the proprietor.

"Two francs fifty."

The other man had forgotten to close the door, and he could be heard saying:

"Is that you, Maurice? Charles, here . . . It's going fine.
. . . See you this evening then."

What was "going fine"? Chave wondered, and he was careful to leave before the man had time to pay for his call. He walked at a brisk pace and, swerving to his right, took cover behind a pile of bricks.

As he did so, he almost fell over the old woman he had seen earlier. Seated in a wheelbarrow, she was munching a hunk of bread. She, too, stared at him—so intently that he felt he had to say something.

"Terrible weather, isn't it?"

But she looked right through him, and he began to wonder if she, too . . .

Whenever he moved too far from the factory, he felt uneasy, because there was no knowing what might happen during his absence. And when he hung around near the main entrance, it was worse; he felt convinced that he was attracting attention.

He had often been on stretches of the Seine embankment like this and had never seen anything noteworthy. Today, however, it was like discovering a new world. For one thing, the number of people fishing was huge, especially considering that it was ten in the morning of a workday and the weather was uncertain. Counting those who were on the island immediately across from him, he could see no fewer than thirteen within a radius of a hundred yards. And one of them had taken his stand—as though afraid someone might take his spot—before it was light.

Then there was the café at the corner, the one on the right-hand side. It was the usual type found in the suburbs of Paris, with a zinc-covered bar and, on an adjoining counter, a colorful display of cigarette packs, mostly blue or yellow, in charge of which was the proprietor's wife. And most of the people dropping in were quite ordinary. But what about that fellow in a blue coat sitting near the glass door, his hat on the back his head, who cast frequent glances at the street outside? He had been there since half past eight, and it was difficult to account for his prolonged presence.

The old woman, who was wearing a man's boots, cracked and laceless, had finally moved away, but there was no certainty she wasn't somewhere nearby.

Then there was the Pole. Chave thought of him as a Pole because he had light blond hair, cropped very short, a close-fitting suit, and in general reminded him of certain Poles he had met in his Paris days. He was obviously poor; his clothes, though well cut, were threadbare; and his shoes were nearly as dilapidated as the old woman's.

What earthly pleasure could the man find in marching a hideous little cur up and down the riverbank, sometimes pausing to stare lackadaisically at the barges?

For a moment, Chave suspected this man might be the mysterious K., of whom he had heard so much. The idea was farfetched. The Pole didn't resemble in the least the description that had been given him.

It was all very puzzling—and disquieting. Why should so many people be hanging around on a depressing quay under the threat of rain? The least thing was enough to catch their eyes. Some stood without moving for a good quarter of an hour, watching just one of the fishermen, and tore themselves away only when convinced they wouldn't see him haul up even the smallest of small fry.

Most of their attention was on the barges, one of which, a brown one, was flying the Belgian flag. Through the crocheted curtains of the cabin glimpses could be had of a family going about their household tasks while the crane extracted tiles from the hold. There was a boy of seven or eight—and the sight of him switched Chave's thoughts to Pierrot. Had it turned out to be measles?

Just then he blushed. A girl without a hat, her apron showing under her unbuttoned coat, a shopping net in her hand, had called to him as she hurried past:

"Not hungry?"

It was the maid from the café-hotel in which he'd slept, and, on seeing her, his conscience pricked him again. He had no intention of going back or paying his bill. He consoled himself with the thought that the bicycle he had left there would cover it many times over.

The Pole had vanished, but that meant nothing. Perhaps he was behind one of the trees bordering the river. As for the man in the blue coat, he showed no sign of leaving the café; now and again he went up to the cash desk and chatted with the proprietor's wife.

Did the police suspect something? It was quite in the cards, and Chave was justified in feeling nervous. On at least two occasions in the past, it had been proved that members of the group had deliberately gone to the police and told all they knew, in the hope of a reward. Chave had written an article on the subject, pointing out that the police showed more zeal in hunting down a handful of decent citizens, apostles of an ideal, than in protecting society from real criminals.

Why had young Rob not shown up at the newspaper office for two days? It was a stupid thing to do; just the way to draw suspicion on himself. The last time he wrote to Chave, he had a room on the Place des Vosges, with an elderly widow who, according to his account, made a great fuss over him.

Often when he walked beneath a tree, a big drop of ice-cold water fell on Chave's face, always hitting him in the eye or on the nose. There were wooden benches beside the river, but they were still far too wet to sit on. The men on the crane stopped working to eat, and the woman on the barge handed them their coffeepot, which she had put on her stove to warm.

Chave's energy was flagging; his self-assurance, too. Indeed, he caught himself wondering why on earth he had come on this wild-goose chase, when his place was with his wife and child in Brussels. Really, all this was none of his business; he'd acted like an impulsive fool.

The authorities must always be looking for him—not merely as an anarchist, but as a deserter from the army. And anything might lead to his detection: a shrewd glance from a policeman, careless talk by a hotel or café owner.

At eleven a whistle blew, and people began flooding out of the factory. Running his eye over them, Chave judged there were about three hundred men in all. A truck drew up near the entrance, and he decided to stay and keep an eye on it, instead of going off to eat, like all the others.

Having just smoked his last cigarette, he went to the café at the corner to buy more. This time, owing perhaps to weariness, he stopped noticing his surroundings, and as he turned the handle of the glass door his thoughts were elsewhere. When he walked up to the counter with the stacks of blue and yellow packs, his eyes were on the palm of his left hand, in which he was sorting out change.

"A pack of Gauloises, please."

"Blues?"

There was a mirror behind the counter, and just as he was taking the blue pack from the woman, he saw the Baron's reflected face. Acting on impulse, he rushed out into the street, jostling someone on his way.

50

Instead of going back to the quay, he turned to the right, away from the river. As he walked up the incline, he tried to picture the exact expression on the Baron's face. What on earth was the man there for?

"The damned fool!" he muttered.

He turned left, then left again, into a street that led back to the quay. The Baron, he knew, was a champion bungler; it was quite like him, on his return from Brussels, to hurry to Courbevoie merely to see Chave and have a talk with him, though he had nothing to say. Chave could almost hear him saying, in his high-pitched voice:

"Well, any luck, old friend?"

Supposing that man in the blue coat was a policeman? And what if the Baron was being watched?

Then a new idea made him stop abruptly. What if the Baron had really important news—of Pierrot, for instance? . . . No, that was most unlikely. Anyhow, there's no danger from measles, he reassured himself; all children have it. After a few more steps, he stopped again. But the doctor wasn't sure it was measles. For some days Pierrot had been complaining of pains in his stomach. I wonder . . .

He glanced over his shoulder to make sure the Baron wasn't following. No, there was nobody in sight. The men who worked the crane were still eating, sitting on a heap of bricks under a tarpaulin they had stretched over their heads on wooden posts.

Chave felt increasingly nervous. The more he puzzled over the Baron's presence here in Courbevoie, the more inexplicable it seemed. Such conduct ran counter to all the precautions enjoined by the group on its members.

He hadn't noticed, but now he felt sure the Baron had been carrying that ridiculous fat briefcase, which made him look like an insurance agent or a salesman.

A clock struck noon, and factory whistles sounded on all sides. Chave decided to leave the riverbank for a while, and made his way to a narrow street parallel with it, where he had noticed a small restaurant patronized by truck drivers. Actually, when he entered, there were no drivers; only a gang of bricklayers, who must work in the vicinity, in dirty work clothes, their faces splashed with cement.

The red-haired inspector, whose name was Meulemans, and who, because he hadn't a hair left in the center of his crown, never took his hat off, had come back. He seemed to regard this second visit as quite natural—as natural as the doctor's visit. He had rapped on the door with his knuckles and said in a genial way:

"Well, here I am again!" With a quite amiable smile, he'd glanced toward the tiny bedroom, and asked:

"Is he better?"

As a matter of fact, Pierrot showed such improvement that the doctor was beginning to doubt that it was measles after all.

"Well, what do you want now?" asked Marie sullenly.

"Don't take it like that, madame. If you think I enjoy this sort of thing, you're much mistaken. But a fellow's got to do his job, doesn't he, like it or not?"

His tone was friendly. He was obviously trying to be pleasant, and as he marched into the dining room, he sniffed the air and remarked:

"Well, I must say it smells good here!"

Marie had just finished eating, and a plate with the remains of a chop sat on a corner of the kitchen table. When the inspector arrived, she was about to start washing the dishes.

"Strange customer—isn't he?—your friend the Baron."

As he spoke he took off his coat, folded it carefully, with the lining outside, and at last brought himself to take off his hat. With a grin, he pointed to his bald spot.

"See that? To think there're some who say we have an easy time in the police! What with the worry and the work . . . But you have no reason to look at me like that. You know quite well I'm here only because it's my duty, and . . ."

"Have you any news of my husband?"

"The next best thing. You must admit I'm not such a monster, after all. I could easily keep my mouth shut, or tell you some story or other. . . . Yes, we *almost* have news of him."

"Where is he?"

"You probably know that better than I do. . . . But I'll tell you how things stand. When we went to the theater, they told us he left in the middle of the show, taking a bicycle with him. It was about eleven. Well, we made inquiries at the station and found that only one bicycle had been booked about that time, and it was on the Mons train." His elbows on the table, he was carefully filling a meerschaum pipe. "Which means, in my opinion, that he's gone to France. If he intended to stay in Mons, there was no point in taking a bicycle with him. Anyhow, we'll know by tonight."

"How can you be sure?"

She had her apron on; her face was lined with worry, and she hadn't troubled to tidy her hair when the inspector rang.

"That would be telling!" He smiled, and added: "Still, there's really no harm in letting you know. One of my men is watching your door, and you can't move a step without our knowing. . . . Well, after I'd seen the Baron off at the station, I called Paris, and they certainly assigned someone to follow him, from the border on. . . . But you have no need to cry about it."

"I'm not crying."

"Perhaps not, but you look as if you might at any moment. . . . Anyhow, don't blame me. It's not my fault; I'm acting under orders. Won't you sit down?"

"I'd rather stand."

"I've come back because Paris had a long talk with us over the phone, and there are some papers I'd like to have another look at."

The day before, there had been an unpleasant incident. Marie had forgotten to buy potatoes, and when she went down, for the second time, she found the old woman who owned the house lying in wait for her.

"I have something here for you," the woman said, thrusting an envelope into her hand.

It contained a letter giving the Chaves notice to leave at the end of the month.

"But, madame . . . I don't understand."

The old creature bristled and said in a haughty tone:

"And let me tell you this, Madame Chave. From now on, I absolutely refuse to have anything to do with you or Monsieur Chave. . . . I had two sons killed in the war."

Inspector Meulemans seemed to have settled down at her husband's table for a long period of work. He had placed beside his notebook a pack of a Belgian tobacco mixture and a matchbox. Opening a drawer, he found some French tobacco, given to Chave by friends from Paris who had come to see him the previous week.

"Mind if I take a pipeful?" he asked pleasantly.

Nothing in his manner suggested that anything serious

was wrong. Though getting people sent to jail was his occupation, Meulemans seemed not to have the slightest animosity toward presumed culprits, still less toward their wives. And it was apparent that he approved of Marie from the way he looked at her; perhaps that was because so many women in her position would have made scenes, weeping and imploring, and she did nothing of the kind.

"I won't ask you if you've had news from your husband in the last twenty-four hours, because I know you haven't. You've been under observation all that time. Still, if you have any idea exactly what's in the wind, you'd do well to tell me."

"What kind of thing would be 'in the wind,' as you call it?"

"You don't expect me to believe your husband dashed off to Paris just for a change of air, considering the risk he's running if he's caught in France again!"

"But perhaps he hasn't gone to France."

"And the Baron—it's equally unlikely he came to Brussels just to pass the time of day with your husband."

Obviously pleased with the ironic tone of his last two remarks, the inspector added another in the same vein.

"And it wasn't just to exercise his leg muscles that your husband took a bicycle with him."

Marie felt like she was living in a dream as she gazed down at the man's bald head, with its fringe of red hair wreathed in tobacco smoke, and saw him, comfortably seated in her husband's chair, looking so perfectly at home he might have been an old, familiar friend or a member of the family.

"You said a moment ago," she began in a thoughtful voice, "that there was . . . something in the wind. . . ."

"That's right. And it's not just an idea. The Paris Sûreté received an anonymous letter a few days ago saying that anarchists were planning a violent action this week. Feelings are running high there, you know, because of the strikes. . . ."

"Pierre would never get involved in anything like that," she said earnestly.

"Then why has he gone to France?"

"He hasn't gone to France."

"Have it your own way! But tell me, then: why did he leave Brussels?"

"Oh, do stop badgering me! I've had enough of it, and I have my housework to attend to."

She ran out of the room, banging the door, and spent some minutes in the kitchen before she went to the bedroom where her small son was asleep. Several times after that, she put her ear to the dining-room door and listened, but the only sound was the rustle of paper or an occasional sigh from Meulemans.

It was nearly four when, at last, he came out of the dining room, followed by a cloud of smoke.

"Still angry with me?" He smiled. When she made no reply, he continued:

"I hope not, because I'm going to ask you to be very nice and make me a small cup of coffee. You're not obliged to, of course. But I have a good two hours' work still ahead of me."

After some hesitation, she decided to do as he asked. When she entered the dining room, she found him seated again at the table, copying whole pages of her husband's manuscript. She noticed that he hadn't forgotten to put more coal in the stove.

"Thanks. It's most kind of you. . . . I hope you haven't got the idea . . ." He broke off, but she guessed that he was on the point of adding, "that this sort of job appeals to me." He seemed fond of harping on this theme, and she was half inclined to think he meant it.

She said emphatically:

"Pierre isn't the kind of man you imagine. He wouldn't harm a fly!"

"I daresay not. It isn't flies he's after."

"I suppose you think that's clever."

"I don't think anything," he said, sounding sulky.

She had wanted to make him talk, but once more they had disagreed almost at once. She went back to the bedroom and began darning her husband's socks. By six, she could bear it no longer and, after a perfunctory knock, opened the dining-room door.

"Haven't you finished yet? . . . I must say, you've made a nice mess, with your ashes all over the place. Do you expect me to clean up?"

He blushed a little, apologized, and began scooping up the shreds of tobacco and the ashes scattered over the table.

"Anyhow," he said, "let me give you a piece of sound advice. Get him to come back to Belgium, if you possibly can."

"But I've told you . . ."

"I know what you've told me. But perhaps, if you think it over, you may find some way of getting in touch with him. Mind you, I'm speaking in your interest. It doesn't matter to me one way or the other. I'll send in my report, and after that it will be up to the French police. . . . But I warn you, if he lets himself get caught—and he's bound to be caught if he stays long enough—he's a goner."

"What do you mean by that?"

"That the French are pretty easygoing on some crimes, but they draw the line at bombs."

"But my husband . . ."

"Your husband left just when they're expecting a violent act to take place. The letters I've been copying show that he's been closely involved with this French anarchist group, giving them advice. In fact, he's a sort of leader."

"I assure you . . ."

The people in the house opposite, told by the old woman downstairs what was going on, could be seen peeping through their curtains, and that evening they left their shutters open much later than usual.

"It was very kind of you to provide that cup of coffee. Remember, if I'm giving you this advice, it's for your own good."

Horrified as she was by what Meulemans had told her, Marie let him go without making any promise. He tramped down the stairs, and there was an interval of a minute or more before the street door closed—which meant that the old woman had buttonholed him on his way out.

Before lighting the lamps, Marie went to the window. She noticed a man's dim form in the doorway of the house opposite. He was reading a newspaper by the light from the street lamp, but he kept glancing across toward her.

There was a creak in the next room. Pierrot had moved in bed, and his mother expected to hear a small voice whimpering: "Thirsty!"

But when she went to look at him, he was asleep. A dream had made him restless, and, as she bent over, she heard him murmur in his sleep:

"Don't want to, Mama."

What was it he didn't want to do? What could he be dreaming?

She pulled down the blinds and, after turning on the table lamp, saw that Meulemans, nothing if not orderly, had replaced Pierre's papers exactly as they were before.

4

TOWARD THREE IT was as if a heavy blanket had been lifted, and one could breathe more freely. All day, till now, the clouds had hung so low over Paris as to seem to brush the housetops, but now they were billowing up toward the zenith, a golden glow shone through, and people were conscious of the sun behind them. The houses, too, seemed to recede, giving a sense of spaciousness; the streets looked wider; barges that had been mere dark blurs all morning, hardly distinguishable from the water, stood out in clear relief, and sudden gleams of light dappled the surface of the river.

Walking past the corner café, Chave glanced in; neither the man in blue nor the Baron was to be seen. Oddly, though the weather had improved, there were only half as many fishermen as in the morning, and the old woman seemed to have disappeared for good.

These trivial observations, coupled with the fact that he

had just eaten and had two cups of coffee laced with rum, restored, to some extent, Chave's self-confidence. Still, he had to admit that his first attempts to exercise it had proved a fiasco.

The factory's gatekeeper was taking his Alsatian for another walk, but this time down near the water, where the animal could stop to sniff a tree trunk every twenty yards. Sunbeams were beginning to pierce the clouds, and every now and then a flurry of drops would glitter down from high branches.

"Nice-looking dog," Chave had remarked affably to the man, who was standing still while his dog investigated a tree. "Is he good-tempered?"

First the man gave him a long, slow look, from head to foot, pausing at certain details of his appearance, such as the missing button on his raincoat; then, without a word, he turned on his heel and crossed the street, whistling to his dog.

"Come along!"

Trivial as this rebuff was, it was enough to reduce Chave's spirits to their lowest ebb. An eerie change seemed to come over the scene around him; there was something sinister about the dingy, rusty leaves, the slow-moving water flecked with bubbles, the almost deserted island with its deceptive likeness to real countryside.

The Belgian bargeman was sitting at the stern of his boat, watching the men working the crane. With a faraway look in his placid blue eyes, he seemed the picture of contentment. It made Chave almost angry with himself: why couldn't he be like other men and make the best of things, instead of always pining for a better world?

The incident with the dog still rankled. The dog had seemed friendly enough; not so its master. Chave had ad-

61

dressed him amiably, had made an opening for an exchange of views on things in general. Had the man been less stupid or cantankerous, something might have happened. He might have said: "You're the gatekeeper at the factory, aren't you? Well, I happen to know that there's a plot to plant a bomb there, and dozens of people may lose their lives—you, too, likely as not. Now if we put our heads together, you and I . . ."

He smiled bitterly. If he'd spoken that way, the man would merely have eyed him still more suspiciously, taken him for a lunatic, if not a member of a gang of criminals, and quite possibly sent for the police.

So why should he go on taking all this worse than futile trouble, risking his freedom on a fool's errand? His clothes were damp, and he was susceptible to chill. Once he'd gotten a cold, it usually lasted all winter.

Suddenly his heart almost missed a beat. He was looking toward the bridge, and a bicycle had just appeared on it, threading its way between the trucks. It was ridden by a young man wearing a cloth cap, who turned at the end of the bridge and came along the street beside the river. As he rode past the factory, he gave it a quick glance before speeding off in the direction of the Neuilly bridge.

If Chave had had his bicycle, he would have gone in pursuit, because the rider was none other than young Rob. Just then there was a lull; the setting sun broke through the clouds, flooding the quay with soft, mellow light. And just then, too, a sense of impotence came over Chave; he lost all faith in his ability to accomplish his mission.

Robert was wearing, as usual, a tattered, wide-peaked cap, and a coat too big for him, like all the hand-me-downs given him by compassionate friends. Obviously he had come here to survey the scene of the operation. And he would certainly return.

Had he not been alone, Chave would have angrily launched into a tirade against the invincible folly of mankind. Couldn't men ever learn to keep peace among themselves? There, before his eyes, were harmless fishermen, each of whom seemed to be a "regular," with steps cut in the clay soil leading down to the point by the river where he fished. Then there was the Belgian seated on his barge and placidly smoking a clay pipe. Others were having drinks in cafés, driving cars or trucks, or basking in the last rays of the setting sun. And there was one who, in passing, had deliberately looked for the best place to plant a bomb!

He shivered. Perhaps because his clothes were newly damp, since a dank mist was rising from the river. He had, moreover, been unwise enough to sit on a wet stone bench.

As darkness fell on the river and the street, all kinds of thoughts were floating through his mind, mostly unpleasant ones. It was as if he searched his memory for them—episodes in his past like that absurd one a short while ago, when he'd spoken to the owner of the dog, only even more galling: things that invited him to scorn the whole human race. He turned up the collar of his coat and thrust his hands deep in his pockets.

At this same time, reference was being made to him by certain officials in the Ministry of the Interior. These men were "in conference," as they put it, in a huge gloomy room, the walls of which were adorned with portraits of dead officials and commemorative prints. They were gazing anxiously at one another across an enormous table. Sometimes they jotted notes on pads in front of them.

"So the writer of the anonymous letter has not been traced?"

"No. He's evidently a member of the gang, but I doubt he's one of our regular informers."

"You don't think it's a false alarm?"

"No, I don't. For some time now, there's been unusual activity in anarchist circles; that much we know. Also, several foreign agitators have come to Paris recently."

"Have you any idea when it's going to take place?"

"Tomorrow or the next day, probably; anyhow, in the course of the week. Needless to say, we're keeping an eye on all the members of this group. Some valuable information has come to us from Brussels. A man called 'the Baron' went there to confer with Chave, a deserter who writes in anarchist periodicals. Chave left Brussels at once, and we assume he's now in France. One of our men followed the Baron from the border, and his report has just come in. It seems that the Baron is hanging around near the Courbevoie bridge. And that's within a hundred yards of the Roche factory."

All of this passed in an atmosphere of departmental calm. Outside the room, a flunky with a silver chain around his neck warned visitors off with the announcement, "The gentlemen are in conference."

"I have detailed four plainclothesmen to keep watch there, at different points. . . ."

Now that it was quite dark, Chave rose, ran his hand across his forehead, and frowned at the streetlights strung out in glimmering perspective along the river.

It struck him that a hot drink would make him feel better, so he went, not to the café on the corner, but to a smaller one nearby. He had no special reason for this, except that it would be a change. He went up to the bar, rested his elbows on it, and asked for coffee. Then he glanced carelessly around the room.

There was a noisy game of cards in progress at a corner table. Suddenly two pairs of eyes made contact, and it was like a clash of fists. One of the four players, the biggest and most boisterous, was none other than the Baron.

The man's first reaction was one of embarrassment; he stopped short in the middle of a story and blushed, as he always did when caught in an indiscretion. He fully realized that what he was doing now—playing cards with total strangers in a café a stone's throw from the airplane-parts factory—was, to say the least, rash. Moreover, Chave made no secret of his annoyance; he frowned heavily and his look said as clearly as words, Well, of all the blundering fools . . . !

A minute later, after he'd drunk his coffee, he followed the look with a discreet but peremptory gesture, meaning: Get out at once!

He slammed his money on the bar and stalked out, raging inside. He had been badly shaken by the encounter and walked quickly alongside the dark river, casting glances over his shoulder to see if he was being followed. When he had gone about fifty yards, he heard the tinkle of the café's doorbell and saw a burly form emerge.

He walked faster, taking cover behind trees as much as he could, hoping the Baron wouldn't notice him, would cross the bridge, and leave the danger zone without delay.

But, to Chave's annoyance, the wretched man caught sight of him and started in his direction at a shambling trot. Only the fear of drawing attention to himself prevented Chave from breaking into a run. With no hope of shaking the Baron off, he decided to wait for him, and moved behind a stack of bricks. He could hear the man puffing and blowing as he always did with the least exertion.

"Gone really crazy, have you?" he exclaimed.

"Ssh! Look, I have something to tell you."

"What?"

"The Belgian police have searched your place. They know you've come to France."

"They didn't arrest you?"

"No."

"And you were fool enough to come here, of all places! Don't you realize they've been following you the whole time? That's why they let you go, of course, and that's why . . ."

He stopped abruptly. Something had moved behind the third or fourth tree of the row along the bank. Quickly, he took to his heels. Though he hadn't actually seen anyone, he was now convinced that the police were here in force. He had noticed an alley on the right that led into a tangle of small streets. Once around the corner, he stopped and listened. There was no sound but the thudding of his heart.

Actually, though of course Chave was unaware of it, the police inspector behind the tree was alone. He'd had to go call headquarters for reinforcements. So far, none had turned up. His instructions were not to let the Baron out of his sight, and for this reason he had made no attempt to follow Chave.

Now, he decided, the time had come for action. He walked quickly up to the Baron.

"What do you want?" the fat man asked querulously. He'd known at once that the man was a policeman.

"Who was that fellow?"

"What fellow?"

"Don't play dumb. That fellow you were talking to just now."

"I wasn't talking to anybody."

"Have it your own way. Hold out your wrists."

"But . . ."

"There's no 'but' about it. Hand over that briefcase. I'll look after it."

And, less than a hundred yards from the bridge, where people and cars were crossing in a steady stream, handcuffs clicked around the Baron's wrists.

"Now come along with me. And if you try any tricks, or make a noise, you'll be sorry for it." The inspector glanced at his watch. In a quarter of an hour at most, reinforcements from the district police station would be here.

When the Baron began protesting again, he added:

"No nonsense, now. We don't want everybody looking at us."

They walked along the river, through patches of light and shade, their forms merging every twenty yards or so into the dark bulk of a tree trunk, swerving around stacks of bricks, changing direction at the bridge approaches.

"So you still refuse to say who it was?"

"I never saw him before."

"Have it your own way," the policeman repeated. "But perhaps you'll sing a different tune when the super has you on the mat."

The inspector was a Corsican with bushy black eyebrows. He seemed bored by what he was doing.

Just then a small, stout man with a gray felt hat got off a bus, and the inspector gave a low whistle to attract his attention. The small man walked up to the Baron and his captor, and, because of the darkness, peered at them closely.

"Ah, it's you. I wasn't at headquarters when the call

came through, but . . ." He stopped abruptly; his eyes had fallen on the handcuffs. His gaze moved up to the Baron's fat pink face.

"Who is it?" he asked the inspector.

"A fellow I took over at the border. I've followed him here. I thought I'd get in touch with the gang that way, but he spoke to only one man—a few minutes ago—who got away before I had a chance to see him properly."

A taxi stopped, and a man got out.

"Here's the super," said the small man.

"Good. Go tell him I'm here."

A moment later there were three of them around the Baron, on the dimly lighted quay.

"So you couldn't identify the other man?" the superintendent said irritably.

"I didn't get near enough. All I can say is that he was wearing a tan raincoat, and he must be pretty young, because he can run like a hare."

"Stay here. I'll call headquarters."

His chief, not being on the spot, didn't realize the difficulties, and upbraided him.

"Why didn't you bring him here right away? Hanging around on the quay won't help. Shove him in a taxi, and we'll see if we can't make him talk."

When the superintendent returned to the three men, a taxi accompanied him, and he told the Baron to get in. To the two plainclothesmen, he said:

"Don't let yourselves be seen together. Keep your eyes open and stay around here till I come back."

The Corsican was still holding the Baron's briefcase. He ran after the taxi and pushed it through the window. Coming back, he asked the other inspector:

"Well, what's our next move?"

But his companion had no more idea than he. He merely shrugged his shoulders and walked off toward a stack of bricks.

"No, I won't tell you anything."

The Baron was sweating profusely; no one had thought of suggesting he take off his coat. For two hours he had been grilled. Ten or fifteen people, including a high Sûreté official, had tackled him.

"Do you understand what can be done with you?"

He knew only too well, and this was one of many reasons for the state he was in. He was hot, terrified, and had pains in the pit of his stomach, partly due to hunger. But in the chaos of his mind, one thought persisted: Nothing on earth can make me "squeal." So he went on shaking his head and saying:

"It's no use grilling me. You'll get nothing out of me."

At one point, the superintendent went to a nearby room and conferred with Brussels by phone.

Marie Chave had started undressing, when there were two shrill peals of the bell. It was past ten, and she thought the sound would wake everybody in the street. For a moment she made no move, but two more rings sounded, and, putting on her dress again, she opened the window and peered down into the dark street.

"Who's there?"

"It's I."

She recognized Meulemans' voice, and answered sulkily:

"All right. I'm coming down."

"Mama!" wailed the small boy, who had waked up with a start.

"Keep quiet. I'll be back in a minute. Don't toss around and get uncovered."

She ran down the stairs and, when she opened the door, was greeted by the red-haired inspector like an old friend.

"Sorry to disturb you at such an hour. I hope you hadn't gone to bed."

"I was just going. Why are you here? Is there news?"

There was a sound of whispering in the room on the right occupied by the old couple who owned the house.

"Let's go upstairs."

"I'll just see if my son is all right."

Even more familiar, he followed her, and bent over Pierrot's bed.

"Well, how's our young rascal getting along? Feeling better today?"

"Who are you?"

"Don't be frightened. I'm not going to eat you."

"Who is he, Mama?"

"Ssh! Go to sleep now."

She led the way into the dining room, as she did so, fastening the top of her dress, which she hadn't had time to hook—with the result that the inspector had stared involuntarily at the whiteness of her neck.

"Well, what do you want?"

"I've just had a phone call from Paris. They've pulled the Baron in."

"And high time, too!" she exclaimed impulsively.

"Maybe. But what I really wanted to tell you was that we have some definite information."

"From the Baron?" she interrupted scornfully.

"That I can't say. But I can say this: it's a far more serious affair than we'd suspected here in Brussels. There's evidence that anarchists in Paris have planned a really big

70

coup. And your husband crossed the border to take part in it."

He watched her closely, but in vain. She betrayed no emotion. She merely shook her head.

"That's impossible."

"Wait until I finish. And please keep calm."

"I am calm."

That was so. Standing in front of the black marble mantelpiece, her hands locked on her waist, her head drooping a little, she was looking at him with a sad but almost serene expression.

"If you knew Pierre," she continued, "you'd know he's not the sort of man to take part in crimes like that."

"But . . ."

"He's an idealist. All the injustice in the world distresses him terribly, and he wants to make things right."

"Exactly!"

"But not with bombs! You've only to read his writings. . . ."

"Please listen. I quite understand that you should stick up for your husband. But we now have positive information. A violent action has been planned. It's due to take place this week in Paris—at Courbevoie, to be exact. I'm pretty sure that's where your husband's gone."

She had listened attentively, and her face was now a shade paler. When the inspector paused to study the effect of his words, she gave a little sigh, and murmured:

"Then—so much the better!"

"What do you mean?"

He thought suddenly that she, too, must be an anarchist, and a particularly bloodthirsty one.

"I mean that if Pierre's there, the crime you speak of won't take place."

71

"It won't take place if the police act in time. But, for that, they must have something definite to go on—and this is where you can help us. In a thickly populated area like Courbevoie, a single bomb can cause a number of deaths. And an outrage of that sort might lead to serious consequences, especially now, when the political situation in France is extremely tense."

He spoke earnestly, weighing his words, and there was an almost pleading note in his voice.

"I'm not asking you to betray your husband. I'm asking you to save him."

"He doesn't need saving."

"Surely you know the people he's likely to get in touch with, now that he's in Paris."

"I don't know his friends."

"You must know the ones who come to see him here."

"You're wasting your time, inspector."

"How will you feel some morning when you see in your paper that there's been a terrible catastrophe? That dozens of women have lost their husbands, dozens of children have become orphans—and it's all your fault?"

"It would mean that Pierre had failed."

What a woman! thought the inspector. He realized that his attempts to play on her emotions had been mere wasted breath. There was no shaking her resolve.

"You don't understand!" His tone was almost pleading.

"What don't I understand?"

"Our position."

He started pacing up and down the room, and made a gesture of striking something with his fist.

"Damn it all, *something* must be done!" he exclaimed at last.

"Then do it!" she retorted quite calmly. "*I* won't stop you."

He muttered something she couldn't catch; but in his tone there was as much admiration as annoyance. After a moment's silence, he added, looking her in the eye:

"Really, you'll end up convincing me that your husband's gone to Paris to do our job for us! . . . Well, have you thought it over? I'll give you a last chance. One. Two. Three." He stopped. "All right, have it your own way. When I come back tomorrow, I may have something more to tell you. Good night."

Unthinkingly, he put on his hat, but took it off again, held out his hand, and seemed relieved that Marie didn't ignore it.

"Don't bother to see me out. I can find my way."

She heard the outside door shut and footsteps receding down the quiet street. About to go back to her room and undress, she hesitated and, perhaps because she felt she couldn't go to sleep, stayed in the dining room. Drawing Pierre's papers toward her, she started reading the articles that, until now, she had merely skimmed without much interest.

The café at the end of the bridge stayed open till midnight, though it was almost empty long before that. The owner, who came from the north of France, had Norman shrewdness and, while playing dominoes, didn't fail to notice that customers of an unusual type kept dropping in at intervals, and always asked promptly for a hot drink—which implied that they had been standing out in the cold night air.

The first to come was the superintendent, who adopted the café as his headquarters. After settling down in a corner, he read and reread the evening paper he had brought with him. He was a well-dressed man, with a grizzled mustache. Every once in a while, he went to the telephone booth and carried on a conversation in such a low voice that the proprietor, however hard he listened, failed to catch a word.

The Corsican inspector was the thirstiest. He turned up every hour, stamping his feet, his nose blue from the cold.

"A hot toddy. And look sharp about it!"

He had a trick that got on the proprietor's nerves: when the rum was being poured, he would give the bottle a jog from underneath, to gain an extra tot. Though he never spoke to the superintendent, the proprietor saw the two men exchanging glances, and guessed they knew each other.

The third man, a small fat one, seemed impervious to cold, but he made up for this by his appetite. At ten o'clock he insisted on being served a copious meal. The only meat available was chitterlings, and he evidently knew all about them. When the dish was set before him, he sniffed approvingly and said to the proprietor:

"This is the real thing. You get 'em from the country, don't you?"

Possibly there was a fourth man in this group, but the proprietor couldn't be sure. This was a fellow dressed like a tramp, but his raggedness seemed overdone. He looked more like a stage tramp than the real thing, and as though he had deliberately plastered mud on his coat.

"Closing time, sir," said the proprietor at midnight, when, as it happened, only the superintendent was there.

"How much do I owe you?"

"Seven francs fifty . . . That was a large Calvados you had."

All that remained was to put up the shutters for the

night. Once the iron screen had cut the place off from the outside world, the proprietor remarked to his wife:

"Those guys were plainclothesmen, or I'm a Dutchman!"

Their first victim had been the old woman tramp, who had made herself a sort of cave among the bricks. From this she was hauled out by the Corsican, who, after inspecting her identity papers, told her to leave—but in less polite terms. Used to this sort of trouble, she promptly hobbled away into the darkness, grumbling to herself and sometimes stopping to scold a tree.

The Corsican squeezed himself into the hole she'd vacated. Meanwhile, the stage-tramp policeman boldly sat down near the entrance to the airplane-parts factory and, curling himself up, rested his face on his arms and pretended to sleep.

The small fat man patrolled the riverbank. And the superintendent, who had summoned a police car from headquarters, installed himself in it with all its lights off.

The Baron's ordeal was still going on, and as a result, he was looking fatter and flabbier than usual. There was a reason for this perseverance on the part of the police; the Minister of the Interior, who was attending a gala performance at the Opéra, had asked to be called every hour and told the latest developments. Moreover, the Police Commissioner had already dropped in twice, in a dinner jacket.

"You might as well give up. I tell you I don't know anything."

"Who did you speak to on the quay?"

"Don't know. He only asked me for a light."

He was too utterly worn out to try to sound convincing or to bother about the effect he was producing. All he knew was that he must not give anything away, anything whatever. . . . If he did, he would be in for endless complications; they'd give him no peace until he told absolutely everything he knew.

"Look! Suppose we let you go scot-free?"

"But I tell you I don't know anything," he repeated wearily.

He was more afraid for himself than of his questioners. Robust though he appeared, he had a weak constitution, got palpitations of the heart on the least provocation, and was liable to choking fits that terrified him. He was haunted by the fear of sudden death. A doctor he'd talked with in a bar had warned him to beware of violent emotion.

"You're wasting your time," he muttered.

"Suppose we let you make a getaway, or take you to the border and give you a good sum of money, too? You wouldn't have a worry in the world."

A dirty trick! They had no business to tempt him like this; it was hitting below the belt. It also seemed to show that they understood him only too well.

"Look at it this way. You'd save the lives of a lot of poor devils who haven't done you any harm. And you could go and live like a lord in any country you chose to. We could go up to twenty thousand francs."

He kept silent. He felt like he was burning. Sweat was pouring down his face.

"Otherwise, of course, you're in for it. You went to Brussels to get Chave, and that proves absolutely that you knew what was being planned here."

"I didn't go to get him."

"Then what did you go to Brussels for?"

"No particular reason."

"You went there to tell him about the plot. That's so, isn't it?"

76

The safest thing to do was not to give a direct answer one way or the other. If he once committed himself, heaven only knew what these men might worm out of him. So he repeated stubbornly:

"I tell you I know nothing."

"I wonder if you realize your position. Suppose they're successful, and a lot of people are killed by the bomb. You'll have to deal with an outburst of public anger. It'll be the guillotine for you."

"I know nothing."

"Well, all I can say is you're an even bigger fool than I thought."

A fool? Of course he was a fool—no need to tell him that! But he had sense enough to know he'd better keep his mouth shut. He was dropping with fatigue and longing for the time when they would stop and he could lie down at last, shut his eyes, and have a long, blissful sleep.

"Pull yourself together, Baron, and think over what I said just now. There's a train at six in the morning. . . ."

Meanwhile, the police were patrolling the districts of Courbevoie and Puteaux, questioning all the night owls they met. Once, they pulled in the inspector disguised as a tramp—to his great amusement. The fat inspector was easier to recognize, and the uniformed policemen gave him a respectful wink each time they passed him.

All trace of the man the Baron had spoken to had been lost and for a good reason: he had left the district immediately. At three in the morning he was ringing the bell of an apartment house on the Place des Vosges. He had to ring several times before the concierge woke up. When at last the heavy door was unlatched, he entered a dark vestibule and tapped lightly on her door.

"What is it?" a sleepy voice asked.

"I have something to ask you. Open your door, please."

"Not till I know what it is."

"I must see Robert at once. Will you tell me where his room is?"

"He's left."

There was no light in the concierge's room, but through a window opening on the vestibule Chave could dimly see a bed beside it.

"Do you know where he's staying now?"

"I don't want to know," she answered shortly. When Chave persisted, she sat up in bed and yelled through the window: "If you don't go, I'll call the police. I never knew such nerve! He's a young swine, your Robert, and you can tell him so from me next time you see him. He stole three hundred francs from me the day he left. If I ever lay hands on him, he'll be sorry!"

There was a click, and the street door was unlatched again.

"Please listen . . ."

"I won't hear another word from you! And if you don't go, I'll call the police."

He could hear the mattress creak. The woman was getting out of bed to execute her threat. He closed the door behind him and stepped out into the empty square. There was a low sound of water from the fountains in the corners, and the roof of a house opposite sliced the full moon in two.

5

IN A SMALL street between Boulevard Henri IV and Rue Saint-Antoine the road was torn up. Drawn there by the red danger light, Chave stepped over a rope and forced open a small temporary shed used for storing tools. It was snug and dry, and never, perhaps, in all his life had he settled down to sleep with so much satisfaction, so profound a sense of well-being. At the bottom of the shed, the soil was soft and slightly hollowed out. After spreading two empty cement sacks and wrapping himself tightly in his raincoat, Chave soon felt a gentle warmth stealing over him. Off and on distant footsteps could be heard—police, most likely—but he felt quite safe in his hideout, so much so, indeed, that ever after he was to associate the smell of damp cement with sleep and security.

On being awakened, he gave a sort of whimper, like an animal or a child protesting against being disturbed, much to the amusement of the workmen who had discovered him curled up in their shed. They were still laughing as he walked across to a small café, where he had a cup of coffee and some croissants, regretting all the while the snug retreat he had just left.

There was a light mist, which slowly changed from gray to gold as the sun rose beyond the housetops, and Chave knew it was going to be one of those glorious days that sometimes come to Paris in late autumn.

His reason for lingering in this district was that he hadn't yet given up hope of tracing Robert. He remembered that, during each of his visits to Brussels, Robert had spoken of a girl he called "Cousin Jeanne."

Actually, Chave had learned, she was not related to Robert; she was a universal "cousin" to the group. Her story was a sad one—like that of nearly all the people Robert associated with. He seemed to have a knack of attracting those whom fate had used most harshly, life's misfits. Perhaps it was because his own experiences had always been hard, too: tragic, grotesque, or merely sordid. Never, it seemed, did anything agreeable or even ordinary happen to him.

Typical was an incident that had taken place during his first visit to Brussels. The Printer had brought him to make Chave's acquaintance. Since he had only enough money for his return ticket, Chave had offered to put him up for the night. Marie had cooked a good dinner, and they'd had several bottles of wine. His eyes glowing with admiration, Robert had followed all Chave's movements, drunk in all his words. He'd have done anything to please him.

His bed, a mattress and some cushions, had been made up on the floor. During the night, he had suddenly been sick, with devastating effects on the mattress and the carpet.

The Chaves had had to get out of bed in the small hours to help him and to clean up the mess.

The boy was bitterly humiliated by what had happened, and in a letter of apology to Marie, he had accounted for his lapse by the emotion he had felt on meeting a man like Chave. But after that, they'd had endless trouble in persuading him to come for another visit.

The "cousin" was a sister in misfortune. Though Chave had never set eyes on her, Robert had talked about her so much that he had a good idea of her appearance. She was sixteen, stunted, yet overdeveloped for her years, with the face of a woman of thirty. Robert had met her on the farm near Pithiviers where he had worked for a while, under the auspices of the Waifs and Strays Society. She was only twelve then, but the farmer, a sensual brute, had physically abused her. There had been a scandal, and the case had even been in the newspapers.

A couple of years later, when Robert came across her again, she was working in a dairy store on Rue Saint-Antoine, not far from the Saint Paul cinema.

So Chave set out to find that dairy store. There was a cheerful bustle in this part of Rue Saint-Antoine. Half the street was bathed in brilliant sunlight, and people were chatting and laughing as they dressed shop windows and market stalls. Food of all kinds could be seen: baskets of vegetables, mounds of cheeses, pyramids of canned fruit, meat, and trays of fancy cakes.

Chave discovered a dairy store near the cinema, but, though he stood and stared in for quite a while, he couldn't see anyone in the least resembling Robert's girl. He was just about to turn away, when a girl came threading her way through the crowd and hurried into the shop. He had no doubt it was she; not only her physique, but also the hag-gardness of her young-old face fitted the boy's description of her as one on whom the world's injustice had left its stamp indelibly. When she came out again, a basket of milk bottles in each hand, he went up to her boldly.

"Excuse me," he began. She eyed him mistrustfully, and her puckered eyebrows made her look still older. "I'm a friend of Robert's, and I'd very much like to see him."

"Why do you want to see him? And why come to *me?*"

"Because I don't know his address. I went to the Place des Vosges. . . ."

"He's left there."

"That's what I was told. So I thought maybe you could help."

"Who told you about me?"

"Robert."

"What did he say?"

"Everything. That you were like a sister to him."

"Oh, I see. You're his friend in Brussels, aren't you?"

"Yes."

"Why didn't you say so? . . . Well, I'm not sure you'll be able to find him. He's always moving, and there's always someone with him. You can never speak to him alone. Last time I met him . . ."

"When was that?"

"Two days ago. He was with a strange-looking man, a foreigner. He told me he was staying on Rue de Birague." They were walking side by side. Suddenly she stopped. "There's nothing wrong, is there?" she asked anxiously. "He's not in trouble?"

Rue de Birague was quite near, and there was only one hotel on it, a squalid-looking one. Before entering, Chave took a good look around, to make sure he wasn't walking into a trap. As he went down a narrow hall, a young man stepped out of a small office on the right. He had a pasty, self-indulgent face; his eyes were shifty; and he looked unhealthy, dirty.

"What do you want?"

"I've come to see a friend who's staying here."

"What's his name?"

"Robert. He's a messenger; wears a peaked cap."

"Why do you want to see him?"

"I have a message for him. . . . He's an old friend of mine."

The hotelman peered at him with big nearsighted eyes. Chave, who had expected him to make difficulties, was surprised when he said, amiably:

"Try Number 7. You may find him there."

The hotel smelled bad. An untidy girl with a squint was sweeping the stairs. Evidently some of the occupants of the rooms had left already; two doors stood open, and Chave could see unmade beds and nightclothes still lying on them.

He knocked at the door of Number 7 and waited. After a minute he knocked again. Though no one opened the door, he could hear movements inside. Had the girl not been on the stairs, he'd have peeped through the keyhole.

"Knock again," she said. "I'm sure there's someone in. Monsieur Stephan, anyhow."

As she spoke, a voice came from inside the room.

"Who's there?"

"A friend. Let me in, please."

"What friend?"

"One of Robert's friends."

He could have sworn he heard whispering behind the door, but when it opened, only one person was to be seen, a man who, though fully dressed, appeared to have just got out of bed. He was screwing his eyes up, as if they weren't yet used to the light. After scrutinizing Chave from head to foot he asked laboriously, speaking with a thick Polish accent:

"Who is this Robert you want?"

His clothes were shabby, and looked worse for having been slept in. Probably he saw in Chave someone of his own kind, someone who'd spent the night in the open or in a cheap shelter, since the suspicion gradually left his face.

"Of course you know who I mean," Chave said. "I'm a friend of his, and I have something important to tell him."

"Well, he's not here."

The Pole, whom the girl on the stairs had referred to as Monsieur Stephan, had seated himself on the edge of the bed, and now Chave noticed two long hollows in the sheets, side by side. Moving forward for a better view of them, he could sense the moist warmth coming from the bedding. Obviously two people had been lying there only a minute ago, and had been awakened by his knock.

"You could leave a message. . . . If I see him . . ."

"I'd rather you told me where he is."

"I don't know. It's true: I don't know."

Chave's eyes fell on something sticking out from under the bed; it was a human foot in a dirty grayish sock. Uncertain what to say, he looked quickly away and exclaimed:

"That's too bad! I've come all the way from Brussels to see him."

"Well, it's not my fault. . . ."

Chave couldn't keep his eyes from going back to that protruding foot, which remained quite still. Noticing this, the Pole uttered some words in a foreign tongue and, after a moment or two, a man slid out from beneath the bed and slowly drew himself up to his full height, which was above

84

average. Scowling at Chave, he tossed his hair back, then went to the basin and gargled.

Chave had never seen the enigmatic K., of whom he'd heard so much, nor did he have any clear idea of his appearance. Nevertheless, he felt almost sure this was K.

Taking no more notice of Chave, the tall man stood brushing his long black hair; then he patted his coat and trousers to shake the dust out, while Stephan continued talking to him in a language unknown to Chave. The man gave a brief answer, which Stephan translated.

"No. He cannot say where your friend is now, either. But he may come across him. If he does, what shall he say?"

"Nothing. I must see Robert personally."

"Where can he find you?"

"I'll come again."

"But I tell you, he don't live here. One night he slept with us; that's all."

"When was it?"

The man hesitated before answering.

"Oh, last week."

"Why hasn't he been at work for several days?"

"Maybe he's sick."

The man Chave assumed to be K. was putting on a very worn tie and waiting with an air of labored patience that had something sinister about it. Maybe he didn't know French, since he never said a word to their visitor. He spoke only to his companion, and always in a condescending, languid tone.

"Now," Stephan announced, opening the door, "you'd better leave. We have work to do." After K. had spoken to him again, at some length, he added: "And don't hang around this hotel, please. It might be nasty for us."

As he was leaving the hotel, Chave had a sudden thought:

Robert was there all the time, in the next room, or hidden in the big wardrobe near the door. But he didn't dare go back to investigate. He felt pretty sure that by now the oily-looking young man in the office had been given instructions not to let him in again.

The morning sunshine was extravagantly bright, and heady as champagne, and there was a cheerful clamor in the street around the huge displays of food. Chave found it impossible to collect his thoughts, or to take his difficulties seriously. He lingered, dazed by the light and noise, near a bus stop, jostled by the passing crowd. In a window facing him were piles of herring, hundreds, a whole shoal of them, red-eyed, flashing silver in the sun. Marie, he remembered, was very fond of herring. . . . After all, wouldn't it be better to go back to Brussels and abandon this wild adventure?

Suddenly he swung around and inspected the people behind him. Quite likely he'd been followed—and this time he wasn't thinking of the police, but of Stephan and his companion. Stephan was certainly a Pole, but the other man wasn't so easy to place. Probably he came from the Balkans or the Middle East—from some land of want and simmering discontent. Chave had almost smelled it in the bedroom he had just left—that distinctive atmosphere he knew so well, the smell of squalor in revolt.

How strange it was to think that not one of the people around him—men and women busy with their marketing or bawling their wares, idlers gazing into shop windows, even that policeman at the corner—had any inkling of what was impending! Who could imagine that, perhaps at this very moment, two men in a hotel bedroom might be putting the final touches to an infernal machine destined to slaughter their fellow men? Even that girl Robert called Cousin was going about her day's work as usual, delivering bottles of milk.

Chave had no idea what to do next and, almost without thinking, he boarded a bus that took him across Paris to the Porte Maillot. This autumn morning was as radiant as a June day; Rue de Rivoli, Avenue des Champs-Elysées, and the Arc de Triomphe were bathed in limpid light. A little open car sped past the bus: two young lovers off for a ride in the country.

It struck Chave that it would be smart to get rid of his raincoat; the police had probably seen it the previous day, and on a fine morning like this, a raincoat was conspicuous. Stopping in a café, he managed to leave it there.

The air was brisk, without being cold. He took another bus. It was an effort not to relapse into a daydream. No sooner had he set his mind on the track he meant to follow than a host of thoughts came crowding in, throwing it off course. Trivial thoughts, old memories, pictures of half-forgotten scenes, they were enough to blur the grim reality, to make this business of a bomb, a messenger, a Pole, a nameless "comrade" skulking beneath a bed, with his old gray sock sticking out, seem unreal, a badly told story.

All along Avenue de Neuilly, housewives and maids could be seen doing their morning shopping; in the taxis lined up along the center of the avenue, drivers were reading the newspaper as they waited for fares.

It was annoying to have no news of Pierrot. Still, he was a sturdy boy; Chave had seen to that. He had no use for pampering and had always declared that if he had a son he'd spare no pains to make him "tough," capable of resisting the slings and arrows of a changing world. . . .

He got off at the Neuilly bridge, and when he glanced

along the quay leading to Courbevoie, he hardly recognized it, so different did it look under the blaze of sunlight. And he could hardly convince himself that quite likely there were plainclothesmen among the people he passed, with his description in their pockets.

Three times as many barges were moored near the stacks of bricks. Most were Belgian, with big rounded sterns, gaily painted cabins, and washing fluttering on lines stretched above the living quarters.

From a sawmill came a steady drone that rose to a shrill stridence each time a log was cut through and the teeth bit on air.

Where had they come from, all these people basking in the sun, and as still as figures on postcards? Those fishermen, for instance, spaced at three- or four-yard intervals, some in their work clothes—a butcher with a striped apron, a railroad man with a peaked cap. There were women and children, of course; two small boys of four or five, twins apparently, were in red checked overalls exactly like those Chave wore when he was their age. They walked hand in hand in front of their mother, looking straight ahead with big, pensive eyes. . . .

If Robert had really been hiding in the wardrobe or the next room, he must have recognized his friend's voice. Had he guessed that Chave had come to try to prevent him from committing an insane act? Yet even if he realized this, and took his friend's advice on this occasion, the others would soon talk him around to their side again. It wasn't his fault; Robert was like that—weak as water, open to every influence. Chave felt sure it was these new friends of his who had persuaded him to steal the concierge's three hundred francs.

For some reason, a remark he had made to his father when he was fifteen came to Chave's mind:

"I despise you because you're a despicable man!"

It outraged his sense of decency that a man like his father, whom he wished to set on a pedestal, should demean himself by cringing to Monsieur Durtu, his employer, and stand in such preposterous awe of him. Sometimes, when he came home in the evening, he would say, in the tone of one announcing a bereavement, "Monsieur Durtu was in a bad mood today." And his mother had been just as bad. He had discovered, for instance, that she always dressed with special care when there was any likelihood of her encountering Madame Durtu.

But it went deeper than this. He detested the fact that his father accepted the life he led at Limoges, as manager in a boot factory; that he employed men on a piecework basis, forced little girls to crouch all day over demanding machines, and kept expectant mothers working until the very last moment.

"Why should I treat you with respect when you don't respect yourself?" He upbraided his father with the intransigence of youth.

When he was fifteen and a half, he tried to run away, but he had been wrong about the time of the train and was caught at the station. His second attempt, when he was sixteen, had been successful; he had escaped to Paris.

"It's no use having a search made for me," he wrote. "Unless you keep me locked up all the time, you will never prevent me from living my own life."

His father was still in Limoges, holding the same job. His mother had died when he was doing his military service at Bourges. . . .

He was depressed; a feeling of squalor, like that of the bedroom he had been in an hour before, or of the life of the Cousin, or young Robert, had settled in his mind. And yet, for all this depression, there were moments when it seemed as if only a slight effort was needed, as if he had only to make some simple movement, like a swimmer's, to take himself back to the surface.

Children were playing on the riverbank, and he paused to watch, and listen to the shrill young voices. Then one of them tripped the boy beside him, sending him sprawling in the mud. Chave went on his way, after a nervous glance at a man on a bench, who might well be a policeman.

He walked past the factory again. The dog was chained in the yard. There was a surprising number of cars drawn up in front, and he saw well-dressed men moving in a group from one building to another. He supposed they were a delegation, perhaps from some foreign country, who had come to inspect the factory or to purchase parts.

Did K. know about this? If he did, was it the moment he had picked for the bomb?

Chave hadn't forgotten the snub the gatekeeper had given him when he'd tried to talk to him the day before. There would be no use trying to warn the man. . . . Just then his eyes strayed to the café at the corner, and he saw a small, stout man, unmistakably a policeman, drinking a liqueur that looked like Calvados, and apparently clicking his tongue against his palate with every sip.

If the man were to spot him, Chave could guess what would happen. He would dash across the road, bombard him with questions, and, once he'd got him to the police station, knock him around probably, just for the fun of it. Yet almost certainly the man was decent enough at heart. He would only be doing his duty, according to him.

As he watched people streaming past beside the sunlit river, he was thinking: If, for instance, the man and I were standing side by side in a trench in wartime, we'd surely strike up a friendship. If one of us got wounded, the other would stop at nothing, perhaps accomplish feats of heroism, to save him. For that matter, so would the gatekeeper. And so would that sour-faced fellow at the tollhouse who's always yelling at the truck drivers. . . . And Robert, too, poor boy, he's a simple, decent soul. He's had a tough deal in life, and all he needs is to be treated kindly. Even that fellow Stephan . . .

But that was harder. Chave had a grievance against the Pole, and a still greater one against K., assuming the second man in the bedroom had been K. And yet . . . They, too, were unfortunates, and if . . .

At his wife's funeral, Chave's father had refused to speak a word to his son, who, he solemnly stated, had ceased to exist for him.

Gazing at the tranquil scene—children running along the bank, a small girl playing with a rag doll, an old man who looked like a retiree lying on a grassy slope reading a cheap novel, rowboats bobbing in the eddies—he thought how appalling it was that in the midst of all these possibilities of life and simple joy, poor misguided Robert might appear at any moment on his bicycle, carrying something slung on his arm!

And a few seconds later there would be a shattering uproar—worse, a shambles like that after a train accident or an explosion in a mine. He pictured smoke-grimed bodies, mangled limbs, eyes void of all but horror, and, surging around, a crowd of panic-stricken people, gasping, wringing their hands; shrieking women and, later, frightened children to shield from the truth. After that, a scramble for the special editions rushed out before the ink was dry, with lurid headlines splashed over the front pages. Followed finally by the usual search for scapegoats, recriminations, riots, a public funeral for the victims, with armed police cordons keeping back demonstrators . . .

Chave was almost sure he'd spotted another plainclothesman. And what about that old man seated on a bench who seemed to be trying to hide his face behind a newspaper?

He could, of course, go up to one of them and say:

"You're wasting your time here. Go to the hotel on Rue de Birague, room 7, and arrest the men you find in it. Make them realize what idiots they've been, then shove them over the border. As for young Robert, you can tell him—no, don't bother. Leave him to me. I'll deal with *him*."

Chave was no fanatic on the subject, but he had a real loathing of violence; he couldn't bear to see blood or anyone in pain. He felt this so strongly that after Pierrot's birth—at which he had insisted on being present—he had sworn never to cause his wife to have another child, and he had kept his word. . . .

He had the feeling that people were beginning to look at him strangely, and it puzzled him. It seemed to him that he was behaving exactly like the other idlers by the river: pausing now and then to watch a fisherman, or a barge being unloaded, or sitting on the bank sunning himself. What, he wondered, had they made of him at the inn where he'd left his bicycle? If it wasn't that he had so little money, he might have gone there for a meal.

His thoughts moved back to Brussels, where at this moment his wife was busy cooking, and, under normal circumstances, he would have been in his study, reading or writing, with the door ajar to let in some warmth from the kitchen. He never asked Marie what there was to eat, but he could usually guess by the odors. Sounds would come from the kitchen—a saucepan being moved, or coal being shoveled into the range. And sometimes, when his son wasn't ill, he'd hear Marie whisper:

"Hush, Pierrot! Papa's working."

He pictured the little boy squatting on the floor, as he loved to do, with his toys spread out around him, or else pushing a chair, turned downward, back and forth, making believe it was the cart that the vegetable man wheeled down the street from door to door, summoning customers by blasts on a squeaky little horn.

Suddenly Chave gave a start, blushed, and tried to compose his face, but without success. He had been standing for some minutes at the river's edge watching two men fishing from a green rowboat. One of them, as it happened, was the butcher with the striped apron.

He realized as soon as he glanced behind him that there was someone else, only a yard away, watching the same scene. It was the second man who'd been in the hotel bedroom, the one who hadn't uttered a word in French.

Despite Chave's revolutionary leanings, politeness was second nature to him, and, without thinking, he took a step toward him, smiling amiably. But the man looked right through him, as if they had never met.

It was too late for Chave to draw back, so he remarked, nervously:

"Well, now, isn't this surprising, our meeting again so soon!"

The man was wearing the same blue suit, the suit in which he had slept. He had dark-brown hair and fever-bright eyes. With his hands in his pockets, he deliberately turned his back on Chave, walked over to a nearby fisherman, and went back to watching the river.

He hadn't been on the bus—of that Chave was positive.

The only explanation for his presence here was that he was checking the area. This proved that the Baron's information had been well founded. It also proved he was the celebrated K., or at least one of the big shots of the group.

Chave was much relieved to see that he had nothing with him in the least resembling a bomb. He was smoking a hand-rolled cigarette and seemed to be absorbed in watching the fisherman's float bobbing on the ripples.

Maybe he'd come to help with the planting of the bomb, or to observe the effects of the explosion? Instinctively, Chave disliked the man; there was something sinister, almost evil, about him. But he realized in a vague way that this man and he had much in common. K., too, was a rebel, perhaps a visionary—and had undoubtedly, as a boy, detested his parents.

It was close to noon. Everyone was quickening his pace, hurrying home to eat. Presently a whistle shrilled, then a horn blew and a clock boomed the hour at a distant church. Soon the sidewalks became crowded. Men jumped on their bicycles and started worming their way through the traffic, Indian file. Chave had a glimpse of the surly gatekeeper taking his Alsatian out on a leash.

The cars outside the factory left, one after another. Well-dressed men were taking polite leave of each other, shaking hands and lifting hats. There was nothing to show that a bomb might explode at any moment, shattering the bright serenity of this October noon.

Looking toward K. again, Chave saw the man's eyes intent on him, and their steady gaze was at once a challenge and a warning; as if he'd said in so many words: "You'd better watch your step. I have you covered, and if you make the wrong move, your life will be worth little."

Chave felt the blood rising to his cheeks. He now noticed

that K.'s right hand, thrust into his coat pocket, seemed to be gripping some hard object. The butt of a small revolver?

He looked away. Down by the water, an old woman was cutting chicory leaves, probably for her rabbits, and stowing them in a sack. As his gaze roved up the slope, he saw a man standing on the edge of the embankment, smoking a cigarette, his eyes intent on Chave and K. A dark man, undoubtedly from the South, he was one of those Chave had marked as being almost certainly a plainclothesman.

The butcher in the rowboat was winding up his lines. Diminished by the distance to moving specks, people were still streaming across the bridge, on which the traffic was rapidly thinning. The crane had stopped work; one of the crew was climbing down from the high cabin.

K. tossed the stub of his cigarette into the water and started rolling another. Chave turned abruptly and, with a speed he vainly tried to check, scrambled up the bank to the quay, taking good care not to look toward the policeman.

There was no knowing whether it was he or K. who was under observation. After walking ten or twelve yards, he looked back, and met the man's eyes. Their expression, he judged, was one of indifference. In any case, he made no move, but remained standing behind K., who seemed to be having trouble with his matches.

On the other side the quay, Chave came to a relatively quiet street, flanked by brickyards. When once again he looked around, the policeman had his back to him and was gazing toward the river.

It was all he could do to keep from breaking into a run, but he walked the way one does at night when imagining footsteps behind. He passed groups of factory girls, arm in arm, their heads close together to whisper secrets in each other's ears. Then he passed a small boy rattling fence palings

95

with a stick at every second step, occasionally stopping to spit as far as he could across the street.

He turned at the second corner to the right. The street was unfamiliar, but he thought he saw, some yards down, the restaurant patronized by truck drivers where he'd had a meal the day before. On getting nearer, he saw it wasn't the same one; the entrance was different.

A big stove was roaring inside, making the room over-heated. Sheets of crinkled paper did duty as tablecloths; big cruets, jars of mustard, and bottles of red wine stood ready on each table. The waitress was a buxom, red-cheeked young woman, obviously fresh from the country, who looked quite matronly though she wasn't more than twenty-five.

"It's stew today," she informed Chave as he took a seat. "Do you want a vegetable as well?"

The proprietor wore a blue apron. People were jostling their neighbors for more room, but quite good-humoredly. Everyone ate voraciously, there was a constant clatter of knives and forks, and the tablecloths grew speckled with drops of gravy. The red wine was harsh and pungent, and, what with the added heat from the stove, faces were becoming flushed. From where he sat, Chave could see out into the street, across a row of drooping laurels in tubs along the sidewalk. Facing him was a white wall bathed in sunlight. A black inscription on it read: POST NO BILLS.

Never in his life, he thought, had he felt so sleepy, such a compelling desire to let himself relax, his mind sink into a pleasant coma of no thoughts. He felt as if his brain were clogged and needed to be purged of the accumulated worries and fatigue of the last twenty-four hours.

"Excuse me . . ."

Someone reached across him for the mustard, and after

spooning half the contents of the jar onto his plate, replaced it. Twice the sturdy waitress's broad buttocks brushed his shoulder, for, without thinking, he was leaning back, watching the glass door. He was trying to decipher the reversed name on it.

6

HE HAD STOPPED thinking. What was passing in his mind was less coherent, less definite than thought. From the yellow lettering on the door, his eyes had strayed to the black letters of the notice, POST NO BILLS. The wall was dazzling white, and the letters, which looked like print, made him think of the Printer. Maybe it would have been better to call him.

He was using a toothpick with the meticulousness of someone who isn't pressed for time. Suddenly, on the strip of empty sidewalk outside the window, a tall, dark form sprang into view. It was K.

At least half the other customers were in a position to observe the scene that followed, but none of them paid much attention; and those who saw part only couldn't make head or tail of it. K. was walking fast, and gave the impression of a man in a panic, wanting to run but restraining himself.

The white wall with the black inscription was like a stage

98

backcloth, floodlighted from above. K. had entered the field of vision by himself. Suddenly another man, whom Chave recognized at once as the short, fat policeman, came into it from the other direction.

Naturally, K. saw him, too, and promptly turned around. But as he did so, a third man, the dark-skinned plainclothesman, made his appearance, coming toward K. It 'had the neatness of a perfectly timed stage effect.

What was happening had nothing dreamlike about it, but for Chave, who had just had an ample meal, drunk most of a bottle of strong wine, and, toothpick between his lips, was slipping away into an agreeable somnolence, it was totally unreal.

The characters on the sunlit stage looked smaller than life, and their movements were as stiff and jerky as those of marionettes. Now K. was midway between the two policemen, sunlight falling on his shabby blue suit and his long brown hair, his right hand still in his pocket. The fat inspector, cutting off his retreat in one direction, seemed harmless enough; the dark, beetle-browed one looked to be the villain of the piece.

And within a few yards of the three men, some twenty people were eating a hearty meal, chatting with their neighbors, or gazing into space.

As a matter of fact, though to Chave each second seemed eternal, it was over quickly.

The distance between K. and the two policemen had rapidly diminished. When he realized he was cornered, he stopped for a moment, three yards from the dark one. The sound of a shot was heard, and K. vanished quickly from the field of vision.

The plainclothesman staggered back, pressing his hands to his stomach, and stayed there, neither crouching nor standing, but as if hung on the wall by a nail driven through his coat collar. The small, fat one rushed toward him, but, when the wounded man shouted something, swerved off in pursuit of K., his gun in one hand, the other fumbling for his whistle.

Everyone in the restaurant now jumped up. The door was open. Chave, like the others, hurried out to the sidewalk and stared at the two receding figures. The policeman in pursuit was blowing his whistle frantically.

Some of the people from the restaurant crossed over to the wounded man. A young driver whose taxi was parked a little way down the street, said to a man beside him:

"I'd better take him to a hospital."

He ran to his taxi, started the engine, and pulled up.

"Give us a hand. Gently, now!"

They carried the man to the taxi. His eyes were open, and he grimaced when the man in front stumbled as they were placing him on the seat. Meanwhile, the proprietor of the restaurant was busy at the telephone. Two bottles of wine had been upset, making red stains on the sanded floor.

Chave wondered what to do. It wouldn't be wise to go out into the street again, he decided; the fat policeman might be back at any moment. But he'd better not remain in the restaurant. He could hear the proprietor in conversation with someone on the phone; more police would be here within the next few minutes. He retreated to the back of the restaurant and opened a door he had noticed earlier. A hand painted on the wall pointed to a backyard cluttered with barrels and piles of empty bottles. On the left was a w.c., but that, he thought, would not be safe. At the far end of the yard was another door. Opening it, he found a flight of stone steps leading down to the cellar.

He spent an hour there, sitting on a big barrel, but ready

to slip behind it at the least sign of danger. A pungent odor he had long forgotten hovered in the air, the smell of wine in the wood. No sound reached him from outside, and his only distraction was watching two kittens playing hide-and-seek around the barrels without much energy.

It was a little after four when he thought it safe to make a move. He hoped to be able to cross the restaurant without attracting attention; it would be assumed that he'd been visiting the w.c. What he hadn't reckoned on was that he would step into an empty room. Looking around, he saw no one but the proprietor, who, steel-rimmed spectacles perched on his nose, was sitting in front of his stove reading the paper.

To retreat was out of the question, and so, with an assumed casual air, Chave went up to him. The proprietor stared at him over his spectacles with comical bewilderment, exclaiming:

"Well, I'm damned! Where the devil have *you* sprung from?"

"Has everybody gone?" Chave asked, rather lamely.

Not only was everyone gone, but the restaurant had been swept and cleaned up. This atmosphere of domestic peace made him even more nervous; he felt like an unwanted and inopportune intruder.

"Anyhow, he wasn't killed, was he?" No answer being given, he went on impulsively:

"The truth is, I can't stand the sight of blood. I was so upset that I went out to the backyard and I think I must have fainted. . . . How much do I owe you? . . . Have they caught the man who did it?"

"Not that I know of," the man replied gruffly, looking at him hard.

A quarter of an hour later he was still wondering how

he'd managed it. He'd had to get his bill, settle it, and walk to the door, keeping an eye on the proprietor all the while. Out in the street, he had to fight an impulse to walk fast—anyhow, until he was around the corner. Turning his back to the river, he hurried to the center of Courbevoie, where, he thought, there'd be less risk.

An idea came to him, and the more he thought it over, the more convinced he was that he'd found the explanation. K., who had only recently come to France, was unknown to the police; acting on a summary description of Chave, they had taken K. for the man they had to shadow.

Yes, he thought, there was a certain likeness between himself and K. Obviously anybody who had met them both would never have mistaken one for the other. But he could imagine the sort of description the police had to go on, and it would fit either of them: a tall, gaunt man with dark-brown hair worn "artistically" long, and somber, deep-set eyes.

Quite possibly that explained why Chave had been allowed to loiter unmolested all morning; the police had mistaken K. for him and, the mistake once made, had no eyes for anybody else.

But now, after the shooting, reinforcements had certainly arrived already, and an intensive search would be made in the vicinity. The best thing to do was to escape from the danger zone, which covered, Chave supposed, the riverbanks and the adjoining streets.

Oddly, the last thought he'd had before the shot drove all other thoughts out of his head came back to him: the course was to call the Printer.

He wasn't sure where he was, whether in Courbevoie or in Puteaux, since he had only a vague idea of the boundary between the two industrial suburbs. After he had walked for a while longer, he entered a bar, shut himself in the telephone booth, and called the little bistro in Montmartre where the Printer always ate.

It was a special kind of bistro, one where each customer had a personal slate, on which his meals were chalked up—to be paid for when, if ever, he was in funds—and he was also allowed free access to the kitchen. It was patronized exclusively by a particular kind of men: survivors of prewar Montmartre, conspirators, outlaws. The Printer, who occupied a workshop at the end of the courtyard, was one of its heroic figures. His prestige was due to his having been, as he alleged, a member of the notorious Bonnot gang in his younger days.

"Is that you, Léon?" Chave had recognized the proprietor's voice. "I want to speak to Laforgue. . . . Yes, the Printer. It's very urgent."

He pictured his friend Léon at the other end of the line: a tall, fair, youngish man who always wore a chef's white cap almost as dirty as his apron, which he used for everything—dusting tables, wiping his hands, cleaning plates.

"Sorry. He left early this morning. I think he's gone to the country, since he said he wouldn't be back till late, perhaps tomorrow morning."

"Listen, Léon! I can't say my name over the phone, but I'm a friend, an old friend. Please tell me if anyone's come today asking for Laforgue. Have you had *any* strange birds in today?"

Chave couldn't catch the answer.

"What's that . . . ?"

"I said 'Yes.' Two like that came. I spotted them right away as you know what. I think they're still hanging around outside."

"Thanks. That's all I wanted to know."

So he'd been right! The Printer was under observation, as, doubtless, were all the other members of the group, all probably on the list of suspects. After hanging up, he hurried away. He was certain the net was tightening.

Now that the climax seemed to be at hand, he shook off his lethargy; his mind began to march again. Impatiently, he waited for night to come; it was more and more dangerous to be out in the streets, and cafés were no safer.

That the Printer had "gone to the country" for the day, he didn't for an instant believe. Léon had probably smiled as he said it. Born and bred in a tenement near the courtyard where he now lived, Laforgue regarded even a descent from his Montmartre aerie to the Grands Boulevards as a big expedition. All that lay outside Paris was, for him, beyond the pale.

For weeks on end he would never step beyond the limits of Place du Tertre, where, in a sort of inspired philosophic ecstasy that expressed itself in a prodigious flow of words, he never failed to gain a circle of delighted listeners among the bourgeois at the tables in the little square, because he spiced his revolutionary tirades with Rabelaisian humor.

An excellent printer, he was also a skilled engraver, and something of an artist. Often, on paying him a surprise visit at the workshop, where he slept beside his printing press, one would find him engaged in making prints of one of his etchings, usually an erotic composition made for his personal enjoyment.

He was a typical, old-school anarchist, wore a flamboyant red scarf, and knew all the revolutionary songs and catchwords, and the life-stories of all the leading terrorists. Nonetheless, he had hosts of customers, who came to him regularly for business cards, publicity pamphlets, notices of deaths, and similar work. He cursed them roundly and sometimes hustled them out of his workshop, calling them "bloody bourgeois"—but they always came back.

If the Printer wasn't in his workshop, or in Léon's restaurant, or in Place du Tertre (from his doorstep, Léon had a full view of the square), it meant that he had a cogent reason for leaving his usual haunts. Chave had little doubt that he was in Puteaux, at the group's headquarters, in which Chave had never set foot, though he knew the address.

For an hour he walked at a steady pace, changing his direction frequently and making sure he wasn't being followed. Only when night had fallen did he go to the small square halfway down a boulevard where the café in which the group now met was located. It was a larger place than he'd expected; he could see two billiard tables, and on the front was a sign: PRIVATE ROOM FOR PARTIES, WEDDING BREAKFASTS, BANQUETS.

He stayed at a distance from the café, because he suspected there were policemen lurking near the entrance.

The streets were still crowded and, in addition to the streams of workers hurrying home, a good many people were standing around, singly or in groups, for no apparent reason—perhaps waiting for friends. Near where Chave was standing, the crowd was particularly dense, because, a few doors from the café, was a "Continuous Performance" cinema with an electric bell shrilling constantly in the entrance.

Finally Chave entered a bar, a hundred yards up the street, and, after carefully inspecting all the customers, stepped once again into a telephone booth.

"Hello! Would you ask the Printer to come to the phone, please. . . . What? You must be wrong. Surely he's at the meeting. Tell him his friend from Brussels wants to talk to him."

He felt extremely nervous, and kept wanting to open the

door and see if anyone was eavesdropping. Had he guessed right? Would he hear Laforgue's voice in a moment?

"Hello?"

No answer. Maybe he'd been cut off; or perhaps K. was there and had told the others not to answer. Without much hope, he called again:

"Hello?"

"Yes. I'm listening."

"Is that you, Jacques?"

He called him by his Christian name on purpose. But the answer came in surly tones:

"Who's speaking?"

"C., from Brussels."

"Ah, yes . . ."

It was impossible to doubt it was the Printer, but he was obviously on guard, even though he must have recognized Chave's voice.

"Listen. I know . . . all sorts of things you're probably unaware of. Is Robert with you?"

Silence. Chave was in darkness because he'd forgotten to turn on the light and now he couldn't find the switch.

"Hello?" he said again.

"I'm listening."

"You haven't answered my question. Is Robert . . . ?"

"No."

"I assure you, Jacques, it's terribly important. For God's sake tell me the truth. I must speak to Robert—immediately."

"He's not here."

"And the others?"

"Some of them are here."

"Is K. one of them?" Another silence. His voice shook a little as he continued:

"But don't you realize that we're all in danger, imminent danger. I've been here two days, but I thought it safer not to go to see you; you're certainly being watched."

He seemed to hear a soft laugh at the other end, a laugh of disbelief or scorn.

"Don't you believe me?"

This time the silence lasted so long that Chave thought the Printer had hung up. At last a voice came:

"Is that all you have to say?"

"No, no . . . Hang on a minute. Please." He opened the door abruptly. There was no one behind it; the customers in the café were all in the same places.

"You're all being watched," he said. "The Baron came to my place. The police searched my apartment. . . ."

"Did they now?" There was a note of irony in the man's voice.

"But that's not important. I've absolutely got to see Robert."

"Why?"

"Don't you know what's planned?"

"I have no idea what you're talking about."

"Anyhow, answer my question: Is K. with you there? . . . This afternoon I saw him shoot a policeman at Courbevoie."

"Well, why shouldn't he, if he felt like it?"

"But, you damned fool, don't you realize . . . ?" He could have wept from humiliation and anger. He could guess quite well what was happening at the other end of the line. He heard whispers, which meant that someone was listening in.

Obviously they mistrusted him. Heaven only knew what stories had been going around about him. Maybe they even thought he'd betrayed them; that it was he who'd set the police on their track.

107

"Jacques, I beg you to listen. Unfortunately, I can't come to see you. . . ."

"Why not?" the Printer asked in a tone of naïve astonishment, like that of the innocent dupe in a gangster movie. Chave pictured the man chuckling to himself, and he gritted his teeth savagely.

"For the good reason," he retorted, "that the police are all around you. If you don't believe it, try to take a walk. You'll soon find, if you look around, that you're being followed."

"Ah, so someone's squealed? That's what you're driving at?"

"Don't be a blasted fool!"

"Thanks . . . Have you anything else to say?"

There was more whispering; then the Printer spoke again:

"Where are you calling from?"

"That's not important."

"Pardon me, it has great importance. Some of us would very much like to have a little talk with you."

"They can wait."

"And someone's just remarked that it's rather funny you should know so much about the doings of the police."

"For God's sake, quit wasting time, and tell me where I can see Robert. That's all I ask of you. Afterward, I'll give you all the explanations you want."

His cheeks turned scarlet; he had just heard a sharp click. The receiver at the other end had been hung up. For a moment he thought of dialing the number again; then he changed his mind and stepped out of the booth. As he did so, someone collided with him, and he almost bolted from the place. While he was paying for the call at the counter, he saw the man who had bumped into him staggering toward

108

the w.c., apparently drunk. Still, wasn't he fully justified in suspecting everyone who crossed his path of belonging to the police?

The cinema was right across the street, and the stridence of the bell came to his ears above other noises. Looking at the windows of the upper room of the café where his friends were gathered, he weighed his chances if he were to risk marching boldly across, defying the police, and joining them.

If he decided against this, it wasn't on his own account, but for the sake of Robert, whom he pictured at this moment being primed for his assignment in some obscure hideout, pending zero hour. Quite likely he was still in that sordid hotel on Rue de Birague. Chave could picture them giving him with a glass or two of neat absinthe at the last moment, to dispel any lingering scruple. . . .

There were many small cafés on this street. Entering another, Chave called the Printer again.

"It's the same person who called five minutes ago!"

He had stopped wondering why he was doing this— whether it was devotion to Robert or exasperation with the stupid fools who were manipulating him. Yet he knew them all—apart from K.—and genuinely liked them; when any member of the group came to Brussels, he welcomed him with open arms, and supported him in his service to the Cause.

All were victims of injustice, and loyal to the same ideals he was. And because he had an eloquence they lacked—with the exception of the Printer—they listened, spellbound, when he expressed, in telling phrases, ideas they could never have put into words.

But now he pictured their faces darkening, mistrust and anger kindling in their eyes, as they heard the Printer's account of the telephone conversation.

At last a voice answered from the upstairs room:
"Who's speaking?"

"Is that you?" he asked in a weary, discouraged tone.

"Well, what do you want *now*?"

"Listen, Jacques. I'm speaking from quite nearby. I can almost see the café where you are. I've spent the last forty-eight hours, off and on, at Courbevoie, and I've kept my eyes open. I don't know exactly what's happening, but I'm positive the police are on to you. It would be much better to call off . . . whatever you have in mind. Just now, I noticed two cars parked a hundred yards from where your meeting's taking place."

"Well, what of it?"

"Good God, don't you understand? I wonder what K. and Stephan have been telling you. I went to their place this morning, to see Robert. They're keeping him out of the way, and for a very good reason: they're afraid we might regain our influence over him. And that wouldn't suit their plans. I wonder if you really know what they are going to make him do?" When there was no answer, a note of alarm came into Chave's voice. "What! You know?"

"Maybe."

"And you aren't saying anything against it? You won't raise a finger to stop it? You prefer to let that poor kid . . . No, don't hang up. I simply can't believe that you, you of all people . . ." He clenched his fist till the nails bit into his palm as again there was more whispering. He had a suspicion that it was K. beside the Printer at the telephone. "I came from Brussels," he went on desperately, "to put a stop to it. It isn't the sort of thing we do. Surely that's obvious."

"Is that all you have to say? . . . If so, you can tell your friends in the police that, whatever they may do—"

110

"Jacques!" He realized he'd raised his voice, and was afraid he might have attracted the attention of the two or three customers in the small café. Wrapping his hand around the phone and his mouth, he spoke more quietly.

"Do listen a minute longer. I'm not thinking about myself at all. I'm thinking about young Rob. You know what he's like, a decent boy, and—"

"I know one thing: if they pull him in, it'll be your fault."

"And what about the workers who may be killed when . . . ?"

There was a buzz, followed by a sharp click. He'd been cut off. Chave stumbled out of the booth and across to the bar. There he ordered a drink, pointing at random to the first bottle that caught his eye. He couldn't get a word out; he felt as if he were choking.

Out in the street, he saw the two big cars again, and was more than ever convinced that they were police cars. Also, he could see three men at the corner who hadn't moved for half an hour, but didn't seem to have much to say to each other.

He'd now leave those who believed he was an informer to their fate readily enough. But there was young Robert, the poor boy who'd been sick all over his carpet because, for once in his life, he'd had a full meal, who'd wept bitterly next day over this mishap.

"I'm *so* sorry," he'd said to Marie. "I can't imagine why it happened. Really, I ought not to drink. But I was so happy, being with you and your husband . . ."

One day, Chave was convinced, he'd set up house with Cousin Jeanne, whose name was always on his lips.

He walked away, hardly knowing where he was going.

Suddenly he stopped. A sailor's heavy blue serge outfit, in the window of a secondhand clothing store, had caught his eye.

On impulse, he went in and, conscious that he must be sounding like a lunatic at large, asked:

"Would you exchange that for the suit I'm wearing?"

It was all so dreamlike that later he could hardly recall the appearance, remarkable though it was, of the woman who not only served him but also helped him get dressed. She was an old witch with a vulpine nose and a jet-black wig that looked as if the hair had been painted on her scalp.

He'd insisted on the sailor's cap being thrown in. Had he bargained, he'd have got some money, too, because the uniform was badly worn, whereas his suit, after an ironing, would look as good as new.

He started walking again. It struck him that he should get his hair cut—long hair didn't go with his new clothes—but he didn't dare show himself in the glare of a barbershop. Instinctively, he continued in the direction of Courbevoie.

In his new outfit, it was wisest to keep to the waterfront. He soon became convinced that the police had received large reinforcements. In fact, the whole district seemed alive with them.

Still, thinking it over, he felt somewhat reassured. If they'd planned the action for tonight, there would not have been that meeting at headquarters. After all, it was a settled principle that, at any critical moment, the group scattered, in order to be less vulnerable and to enable each member to establish an alibi.

Was it planned for the following morning? If so, he had a night left and, though he had no idea how to do it, he still might intervene before it was too late.

The notion of intervening had become an obsession, and

now, in addition to his previous motive—that of saving Robert from an act of criminal folly and innocent people from a brutal outrage—he was conscious of another: a desire to salve his own conscience. For he felt personally responsible, in some measure, for the activities of the group to which he belonged; he couldn't wash his hands of them.

How far away, how vague, the early stages of this adventure seemed—the performance at the theater, that absurd morning coat he had been wearing, the complaints of the Parisian actor! Even the Baron seemed unreal, a figure from a fairy tale.

On and on he walked beside the river, under the trees, observing from a prudent distance the brick stacks, the Belgian barges moored beside the quay, and here and there certain figures it was wiser to give a wide berth to. Once he brushed against the Alsatian, which the gatekeeper had on a leash again, doubtless because there were so many people around.

The trouble was not knowing K.'s plans. What instructions had he given Robert? Would the boy come, as before, on his bicycle? Perhaps he'd bring a parcel with him, and ask the gatekeeper to deliver it to the manager. On second thought, Chave judged this improbable; quite recently this method had been used in Austria, so the staff would be on guard. More likely, Robert would toss the bomb over the wall; in which case he'd pay for it with his life.

The air was much warmer than on the previous evening. Memories of the conversation he had had with the Printer were still rankling Chave. Really, if he were to go to the police and blurt out everything he knew, the Printer and the others would richly deserve whatever happened. And, that way, Robert's life would be saved. The authorities wouldn't send to the guillotine a mere boy who had been led astray

113

by older men and persuaded to take part in a crime that had been averted in time. Other lives would be saved as well.

Searching his pockets, he found he'd left his cigarettes in the suit he had discarded. Without stopping to think—so weary was he of thinking, and taking precautions—he walked across the road to the café at the corner.

As chance would have it, he glanced inside before entering. A second later he was walking quickly away. Through the glass door he had seen the Baron seated at one of the tables, sipping a short drink.

It seemed extraordinary that he was there at all, but stranger still was his appearance. He was wearing his usual clothes, and his hat was tilted back, as usual when he sat in a café. But there was a striking change: he looked, not like himself, but like a fake, a waxwork figure, realistic up to a point, yet somehow unconvincing.

Chave would have been hard put to lay his finger on the difference, yet his momentary glimpse had been enough to make him feel that a macabre effigy of the Baron had been dumped on the chair, as a decoy.

Whatever the truth was, the incident left Chave with an unpleasant feeling he had trouble getting rid of. His thoughts harked back to the Printer and his friends, who were obviously convinced that he was hand in glove with the police. How could they be so unjust? And yet—wasn't there a grain of truth in their suspicions, after all?

When, hardly aware of what he was doing, he began to cross the bridge, a picture of the Baron rose in his mind again. *There* was somebody who might easily have given his friends away and been brought by the police to the scene of the impending crime to act as bait. Perhaps because of the fishermen he'd been watching so long, he found him self picturing the fat man in the form of a big, juicy worm. . . .

114

Suddenly he gave a start. Lost in thought, his eyes fixed on the ground, he hadn't noticed anything until he was close to them. Almost under his nose were rows and rows of large glossy black shoes, twenty or thirty pairs at least. Looking up, he saw a squad of armed police in close formation in a recess at the end of the bridge.

His first impulse was to quicken his step, but just then he noticed something else: a big car parked nearby.

They meant business! Only too well did he know the tension in the air of Paris that preludes violence, street fighting, charges by mounted police, and the rest of it. And tonight it affected him more disagreeably than usual, because he had a feeling that in a way he was responsible. If he'd tried harder to get in touch with Robert and have a heart-to-heart talk with him, all this might have been averted.

Maybe there was still a chance. . . . Quickening his step, he walked to the Neuilly bridge and jumped on a bus.

7

THE BUILDING WAS in darkness except for two rooms: the ministry's inner sanctum and its anteroom. In the latter sat a doorkeeper, now reduced to studying the advertisement columns of the evening paper, every line of which he had already read twice. There was only one person waiting; declining to take a seat, he had posted himself at a window and was gazing down at the courtyard, in which three cars were parked.

"They're holding a conference."

"I know. But please inform them that I'm here."

Ten minutes went by before he was shown in. The air was hazy with cigar smoke. High officials were looking at each other across the green-baize-covered table with expressions of portentous gloom, and there was a curious, almost furtive constraint in their manner.

The superintendent who had just entered, still wearing his coat, remained standing at a respectful distance, his eyes fixed on his chief. The minister of the Interior, who was leaning back in his chair, his hands spread on the table, seemed to have to pull himself together before rasping out:

"Well?"

"Nothing, sir, so far . . ."

The minister turned to the police commissioner.

"Don't you think it rather odd, their waiting all this time? Certainly it's not what one would expect. In fact, I'm beginning to wonder if the whole business—the anonymous letter and so forth—isn't a hoax." But he said it in the tone of one who tells a dying man: "Cheer up! You'll feel much better when spring comes."

Just then the telephone rang. He lifted the receiver, then passed it to the superintendent.

"For you."

"Excuse me . . . Hello! . . . Ah, yes . . . No, nothing more . . . Thanks."

Everyone was staring at him. Dropping his eyes, the superintendent said in a low voice:

"He's dead."

"Who?"

"Sergeant Combi. The surgeon couldn't extract the bullet, and—"

The minister cut in anxiously:

"What have you told the press?"

"Nothing much. Only that a suspect turned on the men arresting him and shot one of them in the stomach."

"And you haven't caught the man yet?"

The superintendent looked at his chief, as if to convey

to him how hard it was to explain such matters to someone who wasn't in the police and didn't know the difficulties.

"No, sir. I'm afraid we haven't caught him yet."

"So it comes to this: the Baron excepted, you've not arrested anyone."

"We've just arrested seven men in a café in Puteaux, where a notorious group of anarchists holds its meetings. For the past two days, each of these men has been under close observation. Eighty-three suspects, in all, are being watched night and day."

"And in spite of these precautions this man was able to shoot your sergeant and get away!"

"He was traced to the café I mentioned. That's why I decided to act quickly. Unfortunately, though we searched the place from the attics to the cellar, we couldn't find him." The superintendent's tone was serious but not apologetic; it implied that the police had done all that was humanly possible.

"You haven't gotten anything out of the Baron?"

"Not a word. He was given a hearty meal and all the drinks he could swallow. That loosened his tongue a little, but he gave nothing away—nothing that would help, anyhow. . . . I've sent him to Courbevoie, to act as a stalking-horse, if you see what I mean. I hope others may—"

"You've tried that 'stalking-horse' idea before, and of course it came to nothing. You should know better." The minister's tone was severe.

"I hoped . . ."

"I daresay you hoped all kinds of things. But you're not going to tell me . . ." He stopped himself in time, vaguely conscious that he was wrong, that a display of irritation

118

would serve no purpose. "You realize, gentlemen," he continued in a calmer voice, "the havoc that can be caused by just a single man armed with a bomb. And we don't know who's behind him, how many more such actions are planned."

A startled look came to his face as he heard the superintendent mutter, as if talking to himself:

"We *will* know—later!"

"Later? Really, Superintendent! You don't expect me to believe that you're prepared to let them go ahead, without interference!"

It was the hour when all Paris was stirring again. Crowds were flocking into the cinemas, and two theaters were having a first night.

"No, sir, I didn't mean that. But, unless I'm much mistaken, it's not set for this evening, or during the night. My reason for thinking this is the meeting they had this afternoon. But I wouldn't be surprised if, by tomorrow morning—"

"And what do you propose to do?"

"Everything that's feasible. We're questioning the men we rounded up. We're keeping the others under observation. And we'll continue searching everywhere. No, sir; we haven't played our last card yet, by any means." He looked at his chief. "Who's to go—about poor Combi?"

He meant who was to convey the news of her husband's death to the widow, with the customary expressions of sympathy, the promise of a police medal, perhaps of a still-higher posthumous award.

"I'll see to it personally," said the commissioner.

The superintendent left. After the door had closed, they went on discussing the situation in anxious, despondent tones, and the air in the big red-carpeted room became more and more oppressive as the night wore on.

Chave wondered how to attract her attention. He didn't dare tap on the window, because he was afraid of what the owner of the dairy store would do. She was a sour-faced elderly woman who looked to be a tough customer, and this evening she was evidently suffering from toothache, since there was a bandage around her jaw. It seemed better to wait till the cousin looked his way; unfortunately, she seemed to make a point of keeping her eyes off the window.

The two women were cleaning up for the night, taking cheese and slabs of butter off the marble counters and putting them in a refrigerator, and carrying the bowls that had contained cooked vegetables and mixed salads into a back room. The entrance door was ajar, not for belated customers, but probably to put up the shutters. His nerves were tingling with impatience. How absurd it would be to fail for such a trivial reason!

Suddenly, the girl glanced unmistakably in his direction. He opened his mouth and beckoned. To his astonishment, she went calmly on with her work.

At last he could bear it no longer, and he rapped boldly on the window with a copper coin. It was the sour-faced woman who looked up. After staring at him for a moment, she came to the door and snapped:

"You, there! What d'you think you're playing at?"

"Excuse me, but I'd like to have a word with your assistant."

"Can't you see she's busy?"

He went to the door and called:

"Cousin! Please come, just for a minute. I have something to ask you."

120

Only then did he realize why she'd ignored him when he beckoned: she had failed to recognize him in his sailor's outfit. She still had a mistrustful air as she walked up to him, shrugging her shoulders.

"Oh, it's you! Why couldn't you have said so? . . . I'm going out for a few minutes, Madame Ligeard."

"What! Leaving all the work to me?"

"Don't worry. I'll be right back."

She obviously had no intention of going any distance, because after taking a few steps she stopped, well within range of the light from the dairy store's window. On the point of asking Chave why he was dressed like that, she changed her mind and merely shrugged again; it was no business of hers.

"Well, what is it now?" Her tone was not encouraging.

"Please come a little farther down the street. I have something very important to tell you."

"We're just closing."

"I tell you, it's serious enough for you not to bother about the dairy store. Come . . ."

Impressed by his manner, she followed him to the corner of a small side street. They might have been one of the loving couples seen any night in Paris at street corners, about closing time.

"Have you seen Robert again?"

Somehow he felt that she was less friendly than she had been in the morning, and this impression was confirmed when, looking down, she answered:

"No . . . Why do you ask?"

She was lying, he was positive; and when, overcoming her embarrassment, she looked him in the eye, it was no more convincing.

"Have you seen Robert?" he repeated.

"I said I hadn't, didn't I? Anyhow, that's *my* business."
She turned toward the dairy store, as if intending to go back.
"Hurry up and tell me what you have to say. I can't stay
out here."

Instead of answering, he took her arm and leaned over
her, since she was so much shorter than he was. She gave
a start, and tried to free herself.

"You have some nerve, grabbing hold of me like that!
What do you take me for—a tart?" There was a vulgar
stridence in her voice that grated on Chave's ears. "I can't
think what possessed me to come out here. Let go of my
arm."

"Not until I've said what I have to say. If you knew
what's about to happen . . ." Without thinking, he tightened
his grip.

"Let me go, you brute! You're hurting me." She tried
again to wrench her arm away.

But Chave was beyond worrying about appearances.
There was no great danger anyway; at worst, passersby
would think it was a lovers' quarrel.

"I don't know what Robert's told you, but I do know
one thing: it's terribly important for me to see him. A matter
of life and death."

"I won't say a word until you let me go."

"This morning you were nice to me."

"Because I didn't know . . ."

"Didn't know . . . what?"

"You know as well as I do."

It was exasperating to be talking at cross-purposes like
this, but Chave was determined to see it through, whatever
the cost. Unfortunately, the proprietress of the dairy store
was watching them from her door, and now she started
shouting:

122

"Jeanne, come back at once!"

"I'm coming."

"Wait!" Chave exclaimed. "I think I understand. Stephan must have told him that I . . ."

"Will you stop! Or shall I call your friends?"

"My friends? Who on earth . . . ?"

"The flics. Who else?"

Breaking from his grip, she ran to the dairy store and slammed the door behind her. The lights were still on, and Chave could see the two women as clearly as if they were in a glass cage. Several times the girl looked up from scrubbing the floor, and her lips moved. Though he couldn't hear, he guessed from her expression that she was swearing.

That was something he hadn't counted on: Robert's letting himself be persuaded that he, Chave, had betrayed the group. Still, he had to face the facts; Robert had undoubtedly convinced the girl that Chave was in league with the police.

Without wasting more time, he crossed the street and a few minutes later entered the hotel on Rue de Birague. He slipped past the office unobserved, but on his way up the stairs ran into the oily young manager.

"Where are you going?"

He hadn't recognized Chave in his sailor's uniform, and that was to the good.

"I'm going up to see some friends."

"What friends?"

"The men in Number 7."

"They've left."

"Are you sure?"

"I told you, they left, and that's the end of it. Clear out! At once."

It might be true. Once his lair had been discovered, K. probably thought it smarter to move. Did this mean that all

123

hope of finding Robert must be abandoned? For Chave knew there was now no question of his going back to Courbevoie and keeping watch for the boy near the factory; the police would be on him like lightning.

Depression and anger descended on him, especially anger. How stupid they all were: the Baron, the Printer, K., the Pole—and Robert was the biggest idiot of the lot! Couldn't they understand that violence was not the answer?

At a butcher's he bought some slices of cold sausage and wolfed them down without bread, casting surly glances at the people around him.

Did intuition lead him to stay in the area? Thirty yards away, the light was still streaming from the dairy store's window, and when he had finished the sausage, he planted himself against a wall directly opposite and waited. He was playing his last card!

Such hope as he had almost vanished when he saw the lights go out in the dairy store and heard the shutters come down. For all he knew, the two women had their meals together, or the cousin slept there.

There being no alternative, he continued his vigil. He could see other men standing around here and there—waiting for the next show at the cinema, for a girlfriend, for a bus?

A young man in a cloth cap, who was reading a newspaper under a street lamp, was the first to achieve his goal: he marched off arm in arm with a buxom, gaudily dressed young woman, who shrieked with laughter at everything he said. Next, an elderly gentleman with a gray mustache, who had been waiting for ten minutes, saw his bus turn up at last, and vanished.

When Jeanne finally came out, he almost failed to recognize her. She was wearing a coat of shoddy reddish-brown material, probably from one of the cheap shops near the Bastille. Though she walked with a jaunty air, Chave could see her glancing nervously around.

Following at a safe distance, he lost sight of her for a while when she was crossing the Place de la Bastille. There was another anxious moment when she turned up Rue de Lappe; he was afraid she might be going to one of the many popular dance halls on that street.

To his relief, she walked straight on, quickening her pace, as if in a hurry to reach her destination, whatever it was. Nowhere else had Chave seen so many people lurking in doorways or waiting around for no apparent reason in the dark spaces between street lamps. In fact, there was an air of furtiveness about this street that added to his nervousness.

Suddenly Jeanne turned and seemed to disappear into a blind wall. When he reached the spot, he discovered a narrow passageway and a hotel even more squalid than the one on Rue de Birague. A stout middle-aged woman, with rouged cheeks, obviously a streetwalker, stood near the entrance, ogling every likely male. Chave slowed down, hesitated, wondering what his next move should be.

For the first time in his life, he regretted being unarmed. He had never possessed a gun. All weapons, anything that implements man's inhumanity to man, filled him with dread and loathing.

But he might have K. or Stephan to cope with, if not both of them together, and he knew only too well that he was no hero.

Summoning his courage, he turned toward the entrance, raising false hopes in the woman's ample breast. Beaming on him with one eye—the other was apparently glass—she pretended to open a door.

"No, thanks . . . I want to see a friend who came here

125

this afternoon." Unused to handling a situation like this, he seemed shy. "My friend's name is Robert," he continued, "and he's with some foreigners. That girl who went in just now has also come to see him."

"Ah, then, it's on the third floor. I heard her stop there."

"On the third floor? I'm much obliged."

Again she bestowed on him a glassy smile, and returned to her post at the doorway, saying politely:

"Don't mention it!"

There was no desk or office, and as he went up the narrow stairs he wondered where and whom one paid for the use of a room. On the first landing he had to make way for a couple going down. The man, who was wearing an overcoat and hat, averted his head as he slunk by, but the young girl, who was patting her bright-red hair, gave Chave a brazen stare.

Up to now, he had been hardly conscious of the accumulated weariness from these days of constant strain, or of the danger he was facing. He had been driven, hardly aware of what he was doing, by his own momentum. But as he set foot on the third-floor landing, he suddenly felt on the verge of collapse. His legs seemed about to give way, his heart was racing, his mind was blank. He'd have given a lot for a glass of brandy to help him through the coming ordeal.

Suddenly it struck him that he had only the vaguest idea where he was. He hadn't noticed the name of the street outside and was unfamiliar with this district. And there was something definitely sinister about this nameless hotel. He had not noticed this at first, but now he jumped at the slightest sound. A door might open, so he couldn't stay where he was. Yet he couldn't bring himself to retreat.

Cursing himself for his lack of courage, he climbed the stairs to the next floor, where he had a glimpse of a girl making a bed in one of the rooms. Afraid she might ask what he wanted, he went down again to the third floor.

Quite unexpectedly, when passing a door, he heard a voice say, "What did he tell you?"

Robert's voice! Without stopping to think, Chave turned the handle and stepped into a small room much like the one he'd visited in the morning. Its iron bedstead, wrinkled sheets, and general dinginess were the same.

The first person he saw was Jeanne. She was standing near the door, which had brushed against her when he opened it. Then he saw Robert stretched out on the bed. Only when he looked toward the window did he notice the third person in the room. It was Stephan, and at the sight of him Chave's nerve began to fail. . . .

"Listen, Robert," he began, but his voice was unsteady.

It was crowded in the stuffy room, and Chave was conscious of the sour-sweet smell peculiar to dairies emanating from the girl's clothes. Stephan, in his shirtsleeves, took a quick step toward the door, and stood in front of it.

"So he followed me, the dirty pig!" the girl cried indignantly.

The Pole said to her in a harsh, guttural tone:

"Now it is good time for you to go."

"Shall I, Rob?"

"Yes."

"Sure you're not in danger?"

"I'm all right. Off you go! I'll take you to the cinema tomorrow night."

His face split in a large grin that seemed ugly.

Chave did not speak to Jeanne, or even shake her hand. Without a word, the Pole opened the door for her, then pulled a chair over and sat down.

"I'd like to know what the hell you mean by coming here." The voice was hardly recognizable as Robert's.

Remembering the night the boy had been sick over the carpet, Chave understood. Robert had been drinking. He noticed a half-empty bottle on the table, beside some greasy bags containing food.

Stephan's cold stare veered from the boy's face to Chave's.

"You've come here to spy on us. That's your game, isn't it? Well—"

"Please listen, Robert."

"You don't have the nerve to deny it, do you? You're an informer, that's what you are, and nothing you say'll make no difference. Who set the flics on the Baron when he went to Brussels? And why'd they let you cross the border, with all they know about you? . . . Well? What've you got to say?"

"Try to calm down. I can explain. . . ."

"Explain? That's good! D'you take us for a lot of punks? We know a damn sight more'n you think. Right, Stephan? . . . I wanna know why the police started watching the Courbevoie bridge from the time you went there. Why they haven't clinked you, seeing as you're a deserter. Why you came to our hotel this morning. I heard what you said, all right; I was in the wardrobe the whole time."

"I thought so," Chave said sadly.

"So you admit—"

"I admit nothing. I have nothing to admit. Look, if you'll just be quiet, I'll tell you everything—though I don't much like talking in the presence of . . . of certain people." He looked at Stephan.

"That don't surprise me."

"What do you mean?"

128

"I mean they saw through the dirty game you've been playing in Brussels. You fooled me then, but you won't again. I bet you're real proud of yourself for bringing it off. How many did they pull in last night?"

"What are you talking about?"

"Come on! You know. All of our group who were arrested in Puteaux. You know, too, that the whole riverside's packed with flics. It's all your doing. . . . Stephan, give me a drink."

Chave hardly dared look toward the bed. The Robert he knew, the decent boy he had befriended, had nothing in common with this leering bully sprawling on the dirty bed, drugged no less with rancor and mistrust than with cheap drink. The strident, vulgar voice went on:

"Anyhow, you won't get away with it. There's someone coming here who'll be real pleased to meet you. If you wanna explain, he'll be glad to lissen."

"Robert!"

"Robert!" The boy mimicked his tone with derision.

"Can't we have just five minutes' talk together, you and I? Why don't you stop drinking for a while and take a walk with me, get some fresh air?"

Sure of his ground, the Pole made no protest.

"Ah! Flics are waiting in the street. Right?"

Robert sat bolt upright and glared drunkenly at Chave. He was dribbling, and his large mouth made a red gash—so red he might have been using lipstick—across the pallor of his face.

"Lemme tell you this. If you turned us in, you bastard . . ."

"There aren't any police in the street; at least so far as I know."

"Then why d'you want me to go out?"

"To have a talk with you, that's all. To remind you of certain things . . ."

"That you fed me one night, and I spewed all over your nice new carpet?"

"Don't . . ."

"And, like a poor sap, I blubbered—because of that, and because I'd had a drop too much."

"It's now you've had a drop too much."

"Oh, shut up!"

It was grotesque, like a badly acted scene in a low-life play. Chave momentarily felt like a mere spectator. His eyes shifted to the Pole, who was baring his long teeth in a mirthless smile that conveyed his thoughts clearly.

"Believe me or not, as you like. But I swear to you on everything I hold most sacred that I have not had any dealings with the police. Don't you realize that if I'd given anyone away, I'd have been obliged to start with you—because it's you who tomorrow morning . . ."

With a quick movement Stephan put his eye to the keyhole, to make sure, presumably, that no one was eavesdropping.

"No, Robert," Chave continued. "I am not in league with the police. If I risked being sent to jail by coming back to France—when, it so happens, my son is ill—it's because I couldn't bear to think that you . . ."

His voice broke. He was suffering acutely. If he had to say these things, he wished that at least they could be said with a modicum of dignity, under conditions not so sordid and obscene.

There was something in the atmosphere of this room that evoked thoughts of foul diseases, of repulsive practices. And worst of all was that Robert seemed to feel at home

130

here. He was behaving like a miserable boy from the slums who has been picked up by an older man, now his mentor in depravity.

He was eating grapes and spitting the seeds to the floor. "Go on!" he mumbled between spits.

"Try to imagine how you'd feel if you heard tomorrow evening that ten or twenty people, workers like you, had been killed—and you knew it was your fault. Haven't you any human feeling for those poor devils, who have to struggle just as we do to keep alive under this rotten social order? Yes, try to picture what it would mean—mangled bodies, men dying in agony in hospital wards, women mourning for their husbands, children asking for their fathers, and no one daring to tell them. . . ."

"Spout away!" Robert grinned. "You were always a good talker."

Tears were streaming down Chave's cheeks, though he was quite unconscious that he was weeping. He was capable at this moment of falling on his knees and imploring Robert to put an end to this stupid, humiliating scene, this hideous nightmare, and more hideous fear of the disaster to come.

"But, Robert, you used to be a decent young man. . . ."

"A stupid young fool, you mean!"

"Don't talk like that! Can't you realize that you . . . you're lowering yourself? Don't you know that these people"—he pointed to Stephan—"are simply using you? And when it's over, they'll drop you like a hot brick? They don't belong with us. They're just paid agents of—I can't say who, but I have a guess, and—"

He stopped abruptly. Robert was saying, in a voice he hardly recognized, a ghoulish voice:

"Stephan, shall I bash his face in?"

For Chave it was almost as if his wife had suddenly addressed him in the tone of the prostitute soliciting at the entrance of a hotel.

The Pole looked at Robert for a moment, then drawled, his accent thick:

"No. We wait for our friend."

Obviously he meant K., and, without thinking, Chave exclaimed:

"He shot a policeman in the street this afternoon. A man who probably has a wife and children."

Robert guffawed coarsely. "Good! That's one damn flic less. And tomorrow, lemme tell you, there'll be a lot more gone to join him. Right, Stephan?"

A bed creaked in the next room. They heard a woman's voice, perhaps the glass-eyed prostitute's. After that, a man's voice, slow and senile, droned on and on, as if he were saying his prayers.

Chave could bear it no longer; burying his head in his hands, he sobbed bitterly. He felt engulfed in a morass of squalor, humiliation, disappointment. He could hardly believe that only four days ago he'd been comfortably seated in his dining-room study in Brussels, sniffing the savory aroma that came from the kitchen, where his dinner was being cooked, hearing his small son's voice, and composing phrases that he read over to himself and corrected in a neat legible hand, to make it easy for the printer.

"Crocodile tears!" jeered Robert. "When a man's squealed on his friends . . ."

"Don't you understand *anything*?"

"What don't I understand?"

"Oh, it's no use trying to explain. You won't listen to reason. But if I knew you weren't going to plant that bomb . . ."

"Why not show it to him, Stephan. He might like to see it."

Chave dropped his hands. His eyes were sparkling.

"So it's here?"

"If you had eyes in your head, you'd've spotted it long ago. It's staring you in the face!"

Again Stephan bent toward the door, listened, and cautiously peeped out. Someone was coming up the stairs. But it wasn't K., and the door closed again, while Chave trembled at the thought of his near audacity. He'd been on the brink of taking the chance provided by the open door, shoving the Pole aside, and making a dash down to the street to warn the first policeman he met.

"Stephan!"

The Pole, his lips still set in their oddly artificial smile, looked at Robert.

"Watch out! Maybe he's got a gun."

Stephan shook his head. Evidently, though Chave hadn't noticed anything, he had already taken the precaution of feeling his pockets.

"What you gonna do with him?" Robert asked.

"Keep him here until it's over. Unless the boss has other plans."

"Suppose he starts yelling?"

Stephan withdrew his hand from his pocket just enough to show that it was gripping a gun.

Robert yawned. "What time is it?"

"Ten."

"When are they coming for me?"

"Not before five."

"I'd like to sleep. The trouble is . . ." He looked at Chave and frowned, then shrugged his shoulders. "Oh well, you can manage him."

Before settling down to sleep, he took a long pull at the brandy bottle and munched some grapes, spitting the seeds against the wall.

"Good night, Stephan, old friend."

He had turned his face toward the wall, and his expression couldn't be seen when he murmured, for Chave's benefit:

"Night, you old bastard!"

8

THE ROOM WAS like other disagreeable places: sickrooms, shelters for the homeless, barracks, night trains, prison cells, and death chambers—places that lie outside the normal course of life; places of oppression and constraint, where the air is foul and leaves a bitter taste on the lips.

This was Chave's dominant impression as he hovered on the edge of sleep in a limbo of dim thoughts. He pinched himself to keep his eyes from shutting.

With a grunt like that of an exhausted animal, Robert rolled over on the creaky bed. His cheeks were moist and glistening, his lips swollen, his nostrils dilated, his hair fuzzy as a sheep's.

Chave couldn't take his eyes off him. For some reason, the boy seemed larger than life, like a film close-up. He could even see the pores of the boy's skin, beaded with sweat. From time to time, though his breathing had the low cadence of a sleeper's, there was a slight flicker of his eyelashes, and

Chave guessed that Robert, too, was watching, though his eyes appeared to be closed.

Seated on the rickety cane chair between the table and the door, the Pole remained quite still except when his cigarette had burned down and he lighted another from the stub. After that he recrossed his legs and gazed steadily at Chave through a haze of smoke.

The three seemed cut off from the outside world; no sounds reached them but, now and again, a senile whimper from the adjoining room, followed by a rattle of the bedsprings. Chave was struck by the emptiness of the room; the only signs of occupation were the remains of a meat pie near Robert, and, on the table, within reach of Stephan's hand, his gun, flanked by the brandy bottle, an alarm clock, and a green thermos.

So nerve-racking was this silent immobility that Chave began to imagine he heard sounds that didn't exist, such as the rumble of a train, the intermittent purring of a generator.

He was sad with a sadness he had never known before, as if all hope had left the world and he bore on his shoulders the accumulated sorrows of mankind. Sometimes when Robert's eyelashes fluttered, he would feel his own lids tingle, his underlip quiver.

He wasn't really angry with the boy, and when he looked thoughtfully at the Pole, he wondered if he had any real animus against him. He decided that he hadn't. The man was probably more to be pitied than otherwise; for all his pose of ruthlessness, he wasn't really very different from other Poles who had come to France in swarms after the war and settled in the mining villages of the north—simple, decent folk inured to hardship. His face bore the stamp of suffering, not of evil.

He, too, must be feeling sleepy. One couldn't stay long

136

in this stuffy, dimly lighted room, without wanting to doze off. That, no doubt, was why he smoked so steadily.

Hadn't Robert said that the bomb was somewhere here, in full view? Chave passed each object in review time after time, but it was quite a while before he guessed, and then only because of the alarm, which brought the thought of clockwork to his mind. Obviously—why hadn't he figured it out before?—it was that green thermos standing beside the clock. Certainty came when Stephan, noticing his intentness, followed the direction of his eyes, and his lips curled in a grim smile.

Some minutes passed. Then the Pole, evidently thinking about the thermos, reached out to the gun, and from then on he never let go of it, even when he was lighting a cigarette.

Thickening as the night wore on, the smoke seemed to work its way into Chave's brain, fogging his perceptions. Not only were objects losing their solid outlines, but also the experience he was living through was growing nebulous, incoherent. It was all he could do to keep a grip on himself, but he managed it, and kept his eyes wide open until things around him regained their normal forms.

Five o'clock, Stephan had said. Like a guard coming to take a prisoner from the condemned cell, someone would appear at five to summon Robert from this room. He pictured them making their way through the wet darkness, handling the bomb gingerly; then stopping near the factory for Robert to be given final instructions. At the last moment, wouldn't Robert feel his resolution falter? Wouldn't he turn his eyes, red-rimmed with weariness, in all directions, desperately seeking a way to escape? Like a condemned man's, his breath would smell of cheap liquor, a wet, half-smoked cigarette would be dangling from his lips. . . .

His eyes had closed again. Angrily, Chave jerked himself

back to vigilance, digging his nails into his palms, and shot a defiant glance at the Pole, who was in much the same state as himself. As often happens on the verge of sleep, all sorts of ideas flitted through his mind, logical and plausible but quite unrealizable.

For instance, one way of saving Robert would be to break his leg; with a broken leg he'd never be able to go to Courbevoie and throw a bomb. It should be easy enough; a hammer or an iron rod would do the trick. And he could deal the blow before Stephan had a chance to intervene.

What, in that case, would the others do? Would one of them throw the bomb instead? Not likely, considering the trouble they'd taken to prime Robert . . .

But no hammer or iron rod was available. And even if he had one, he could never bring himself to use it. Chave had always given a wide berth to street fights, because of his loathing of every form of violence. When one isn't used to that sort of thing, one doesn't start hitting a prostrate man, especially in cold blood.

A new thought came to him. Why not do something really heroic? He tried to estimate the number of people in the hotel. There couldn't be many. Ten at most. The woman with the glass eye, for instance, who plied her trade in the doorway—would she be a great loss to the world? Or that old debauchee who could be heard wheezing and whining in the next room?

Far more people would lose their lives, decent working-class people, if the bomb exploded at the factory in Courbevoie. Wasn't it up to him to fling himself on it and set it off at once? He could seize a time when Stephan wasn't watching so carefully.

Over and over again he weighed this idea in his mind, until the words in which he clothed it grew almost meaningless. But deep down, he knew quite well he wouldn't do it.

Suddenly he jumped. Somebody had knocked on the door.

Stephan jumped, too. Robert opened his eyes but, dazzled by the light, promptly shut them again.

The Pole rose and grasped the doorknob with his left hand, keeping the gun in his right leveled at Chave. Before opening, he asked some question in his own language, in a low tone.

A woman's voice answered, and when the door was opened, it was a woman, by herself, who entered. She, too, was evidently a Pole, and Chave judged her to be about thirty. Short and fat, with stumpy arms and legs, she had an oddly shaped body, all folds and bulges, and was wearing a cheap, ill-fitting fur coat. There was an unhealthy look about her puffy face under lavish makeup. She probably habitually overate or, perhaps, was suffering from some disease.

Stephan resumed his seat beside the door. The woman lit a cigarette and, seeming not to be surprised by Chave's presence, started talking volubly. A worried look had come to Stephan's face. Twice Chave caught a word that sounded like "telephone." When he saw the Pole get up again, he felt pretty sure he'd guessed the reason for this visit.

The police were on K.'s trail, and, not wanting to come to the hotel, he had called a member of the group who lived in this neighborhood and asked her to tell Stephan to get in touch with him. The Pole was putting a cap on, his eye still on Chave. He said something in Polish to the woman, who seated herself on the chair he had vacated, and handed her the gun.

After a quick glance around the room, he went out. The

noise of the closing door woke up Robert again. He sat up and stared with stupefaction at the woman.

"What's happened?" he asked excitedly.

"Nodings." Her accent was thicker than Stephan's. "He is gone down to the phone."

She kept the gun pointed at Chave, a finger on the trigger, and he was beginning to think she might fire it unintentionally.

"What is hour?" she asked.

It was Chave who replied.

"Three-thirty."

Robert was looking vaguely at him, and the rancor seemed to have left his eyes. He reached out for his glass, took a gulp, and grimaced.

"Who called?" he asked the woman.

She put a finger to her lips, and, after eying her for a while, he lay down again.

"Listen!" Chave began impulsively. "Do please listen to me. . . . You really mustn't do it."

Robert looked at him listlessly, then yawned and rubbed his eyes. After a while he said, with a slight sigh:

"You know as well as I do that it's too late."

"It's not too late. Think! It's not only your life, but the lives of others that . . ."

"Oh, leave me in peace, for God's sake!"

He lacked the energy to work himself into a rage again. The fetid atmosphere, in which there now hovered the odor of stale scent and sweat coming from the woman, had dampened his energy.

At the moment the idea came to Chave, Robert was watching him, and so sudden was the change that came over his old friend's face that it almost brought an exclamation to the boy's lips. Chave had intended to go on talking, as

140

before, appeal to Robert's better feelings, to plead with him. But, out of the blue, the solution he'd been groping for since he entered this room came to him, without the least mental effort on his part; it was as if a voice had spoken in his ear. He smiled. It was amazing that it hadn't struck him before.

What was it that had prevented him from taking any action all this time? The gun, of course. The gun that first the Pole, and now this woman, his compatriot, held pointed at him.

It was obvious, clear as daylight, that Stephan, anyhow, would never dream of firing that gun. For the good reason that the bomb stood on the table, and there were policemen within earshot, on Rue de Lappe. If the gun was fired, they'd be here in a flash. The game would be up! No, under no circumstances could Stephan risk using the gun.

Chave was quivering with excitement. It was all he could do to keep from jumping to his feet. He carefully refrained from looking at Robert, who could hardly fail to mark the triumph in his eyes.

Right now, nothing could be done. If he made a move, that grim-faced woman would undoubtedly pull the trigger. But Stephan would be coming back and would settle down in his chair again, holding his gun—which was no more deadly than a toy.

Chave shut his eyes, bit his lips to keep them from trembling, and waited. At last there was a sound of footsteps on the stairs, the rattle of the doorknob.

Stephan came in and, as Chave had expected, took the gun from the woman, who went away reluctantly, as if she'd have liked to stay and see the end of the adventure.

The Pole looked glum. He said to Robert:

"It was him. He can't come, but he's given me all the dope."

"Do we still leave at five?"

Chave's original intention was to wait until the soporific atmosphere had taken effect again, making the three of them nod off. But impatience got the better of him. He sprang to his feet so abruptly that neither of the others moved. Perhaps they thought he had a cramp or needed the w.c.

For one, perhaps two seconds he looked at each in turn. Shivers were running along his spine. An agony of fear was surging up from the depths of his being, wave on wave. He knew he must act quickly or it would be too late.

It was over in a flash, before he'd had time to think what he was doing. One quick step took him to the table; his hand shot out and grabbed the thermos.

Hugging it to his chest, he gave them a defiant look, and, stepping to the door, still facing them, put one hand behind him and turned the knob.

Stephan was so livid he looked like a dying man. He made no move, but his hand unclenched, and the gun dropped with a thud on the threadbare carpet.

Chave did not see that. He was already in the hallway. He raced down the stairs and, hurling aside the woman in the doorway, out into the street.

There was a sound of footsteps behind him. Then he thought he heard a bubbling sound in the thermos, and it was then that his fear reached its height. It was a bomb he was holding, a bomb about whose mechanism he knew absolutely nothing. For all he knew, it might be constructed to explode at the slightest shock; it might have gone off when he bumped into that woman!

Nevertheless, he walked steadily ahead, quickening his pace. The footsteps behind had died away; there was no one in sight. At this hour most of the dance halls had closed, but two policemen were still on their beat on Rue de Lappe.

But because they were there to keep the peace among the people coming from the dance halls, they paid no attention to Chave, who hurried past them, still pressing the thermos to his chest.

He walked across the Place de la Bastille. Then again footsteps sounded behind him; they were gaining on him. A voice said:

"Stop, Pierre . . ." Robert was at his heels, his hair tousled, his shirt gaping at the neck. "Listen! It's not fair what you're doing. I'll never forgive you as long as I live."

Chave shot a quick glance behind him. Yes; Stephan, too, was following, but at a considerable distance. He was apparently only halfhearted about the chase and was ready to beat a retreat at the least sign of danger.

Chave walked on down the echoing street like a man in a dream, a dream of triumph. He wasn't walking, he was treading on air. Never in his life had he had this sense of buoyancy, or as if he were wearing seven-league boots.

He was on Boulevard Henri IV, and at its end, beyond two dark rows of chestnut trees, he could see a white bridge spanning the Seine. He wanted to break into a run, but he was afraid it might make the bomb explode.

"Pierre, I beg you . . ."

With shorter legs, the boy had to trot to keep up with Chave. What an adventure it had been, and how exhilarating it was to be escorted through the dark streets—Chave, a man inspired, a conqueror! He started talking to himself, commenting on his feat. "I knew I'd succeed. How, I hadn't any idea; but I *knew*."

There were still mysterious gurglings in the bottle and even more mysterious squeaks, as if some small malignant creature were in it, trying to escape. But he was rapidly approaching the bridge. It was only a hundred yards away;

143

now fifty, thirty. Looking around, he saw that the Pole had given up; he'd vanished as if the night had swallowed him.

Robert, too, was falling back. When Chave crossed the street along the river, he was alone.

Then, just as he was stepping onto the bridge, a sort of paralysis came over him, a final hesitation. To have it finished, he swung his arm vigorously and hurled the green thermos with all his might into the river. It fell in midstream, with a faint splash. Then all was silent.

That curious numbness came over him again, and when he tried to move, his feet seemed to be made of lead. Laboriously he lifted them, one after the other. Suddenly, it was as if he'd snapped a bond that shackled him, and he started running fast across the bridge.

He swung to the right, along the quay on the Ile Saint-Louis, and when at last he stopped to catch his breath, he was a good five hundred yards from the place where he'd thrown the bomb. Pressing his hands to his chest, he tried to quiet the wild beating of his heart.

There was a throbbing in his temples and he could feel the racing of his blood. He was waiting, waiting for something tremendous to happen: for the sound of an explosion muffled by the depths; for a column of water to spout up like a geyser and subside in cataracts of spray.

Minutes passed as he waited, in an agony of suspense, sweat oozing from every pore. Nothing happened. He heard footsteps, voices. Two policemen were approaching, and he walked on, a hundred yards ahead of them, crossed another bridge and saw the dark mass of Notre-Dame looming ahead.

With a sigh of relief he sank to a bench in the cathedral square. His head was swimming, his limbs seemed to have turned to water. Was he going to faint?

After a few minutes the dizziness passed, and his heart

144

slowed down. Burying his head in his hands, he gave way to a fit of violent, insensate weeping, a flood of tears that washed away the evil events of the night. And there was something more rapturous, more voluptuous in this release than in the most passionate embrace of love.

"Is it really necessary?" asked the Baron, but in a voice so feeble that the policeman failed to hear. He seemed to be on the point of collapsing like a pricked balloon.

Hour after hour they had bludgeoned him with questions, worn him down to such a point that he had no will left; he was a mere automaton. Someone told him to sit, and he sat down; to stand, and he stood up; to eat, and he ate.

Then they'd led him, more dead than alive, to this riverside café, and planted him near the window—to serve as "bait," so the superintendent had told him, grinning. As he looked dully around, at drab walls and beer-splashed zinc, he felt he was in a nightmare.

He was clutching the old briefcase containing the two model boats and a sheaf of typewritten proposals for establishing companies to manufacture under his patents. He had his heavy coat on, and his pink cheeks, whose flabbiness passed unnoticed at first sight, gave him an air of well-fed bonhomie.

"A calvados," he said to the proprietor of the café, who was watching him with amusement.

From where he sat he could just see the bridge, the red-brick walls of the tollhouse, a few of the trees bordering the river.

There was the promise of another fine day. In the clear air sparrows were setting up a cheerful din, like schoolchildren in a playground before the bell rings. One could almost

145

picture the trees putting forth their new leaves and summer returning.

Two tables away sat the fat inspector who first questioned him, and who, at the police station, when the others weren't looking, had given him vicious jabs on the shins, to encourage him to talk.

He had had occasional glimpses of the superintendent in the course of the night, making his rounds. There were plainclothesmen in ambush everywhere, and the riverbanks were filled with armed police.

Nobody paid much attention to them. Passersby would look around with mild surprise when, glancing up an alley, they saw three or four men huddled together in a doorway, like children playing hide-and-seek. But they thought no more about it. The usual fishermen could be seen along the banks, though in greater force because of the fine weather. A barge was unloading sand, another unloading coal beside it, and the growing mounds of black and white made an effective contrast. An odd-looking vehicle, drawn by six horses, was bringing a huge tree to the sawmill, holding up traffic in the process.

The Baron had been reduced to incoherence; even the police were beginning to feel the strain. But this did not prevent them from making telephone calls every few minutes, while police cars dashed between the danger area and headquarters. One of the inspectors claimed to have seen the minister's car near the bridge early in the morning, and, according to him, it had stayed there a full half hour.

"You're still convinced that anonymous letter wasn't a hoax?" the minister had asked the superintendent with the big mustache, on returning to his office.

———

Meanwhile, still wearing his ill-fitting sailor's uniform and cap, Chave traveled in an early train to Brussels and jumped into a streetcar at the Gare du Midi.

The streets in Brussels seemed brighter than those of Paris, perhaps because, being less crowded, they gave more space for the sun to play on. They were emptier and brighter still in Schaerbeek, where Chave got off at the corner occupied by the general store his wife went to.

He had less than a hundred yards to walk, but once more, inexplicably, his legs seemed about to give way. He fumbled in his pocket for his key and couldn't find it; he couldn't even remember if he'd taken it with him.

Somehow he dragged himself up the steps and rang the bell; then, remembering, rang a second time. Instinctively he looked up, to see the window above open and a head appear.

"Who's there? . . . What do you want?"

He chuckled. His wife hadn't recognized him in his strange outfit and with four days' growth of beard. He laughed out loud, an almost boyish laugh.

"It's I."

Immediately, a door opened, and he heard footsteps on the stairs, so precipitate that he held his breath, afraid his wife might slip on the smooth tiles in the hall.

"Oh, Pierre! . . . Oh, you *do* look funny!"

She, too, was laughing. In the hall she threw a mocking glance at a door that opened furtively as they went by. Hadn't that mean old thing been telling everyone that Chave had been sent to prison in Paris?

"How's Pierrot?"

There was no need to answer. The door above stood open, and, along with a pungent odor of leek soup, sunlight was streaming onto the landing. Through a haze of dancing motes, Chave saw his son squatting on the floor, surrounded by his blocks.

"Hello, Daddy!" he said quite calmly.

Evidently the lapse of time had meant nothing to him. He accepted his father's kisses with good grace, but promptly rubbed his cheeks where Chave's bristly chin had scratched them. After a moment he looked up, genuinely surprised.

"Haven't you brought anything for me?"

He was quite shocked at the idea of his father's coming back from a trip without a present. But Chave was saying to his wife:

"You weren't too worried, were you?"

Oddly, what affected him most was finding everything exactly as he'd left it. When he opened the door of his study, he found the stove lighted, as if his wife had been expecting him to settle down to work at any time. The linoleum, which had been cleaned the day before, still smelled of beeswax.

"I'm not quite sure yet," he said meditatively as he prowled around the room, sniffing the air, picking up books and papers and glancing at them, "what's the best thing to do. Really, I suppose I ought to let the police know."

"Know what?"

"Oh, it's a long story; I'll tell you later. . . . But I'd like them to know the danger's over."

"Did you see the Baron again?"

He couldn't repress a smile when he remembered the Baron's appearance the last time he'd seen him. How long ago was that? Why, only yesterday, though it seemed ages! What a sight he'd been, planted near the window of that café in Courbevoie—reluctant bait!

There was a double ring, and to Chave's surprise, instead

of going to the window to look out, Marie merely glanced at the clock, saying:

"That's the inspector."

"What inspector?"

"Meulemans. He's been coming twice a day."

Now it was Marie's turn to laugh, seeing Chave's expression of bewilderment. He was even more taken aback when a cordial voice, with a thick Belgian accent, boomed from the landing:

"So the little rascal's quite well again?"

"Yes, inspector."

"That's good news. Such a bright boy! It would have been just too bad if . . ."

He stopped abruptly, having caught sight of Chave, indeed, almost colliding with him. And the little package he had in his hand added to his embarrassment.

"Well, I'm damned!" he exclaimed. Then he added gruffly: "As if I hadn't trouble enough on my hands, you had to come back!"

The small boy pointed to the package and cried excitedly:

"Is that my trumpet?"

"Yes, little man, it's your trumpet, all right. But you'll have to wait. I must have a talk with your daddy." And, turning to Chave, he said: "Shall we step into the study?"

He very nearly sat down in "his" chair and opened the drawer to take out "his" tobacco.

"I'd better shut the door, hadn't I? . . . Well, I must say, this *is* a surprise. I called Paris only an hour ago, and they told me nothing had happened, so far."

"Nothing will happen," said Chave calmly. He was aligning his pipes in a neat row. "Anyhow, I hope nothing will. The bomb is in the middle of the Seine, near Boulevard Henri IV, exactly fifteen yards from the bank."

"Are you sure of that?"

"Positive . . . Perhaps it would be good if you called Paris again and let them know. And you might add that the people they've arrested had nothing whatever to do with it."

He fell silent. A picture had come to his mind of the sunlit quays, the riverbank dotted with fishermen, the little cafés, each of which had a distinctive smell, the smell of a French province, a country inn. . . . Suddenly he seemed to wake from a dream.

"Marie!" he called. "Bring a drink for the inspector."

She came to the door and asked:

"What would you like?"

"How about beer? It's the best drink in the morning, isn't it?"

Chave's thoughts went back to the cafés beside the river, one of which smelled of the South, Provençal wine; another of calvados, the apple brandy of Normandy, and cider; and the one where the proprietor had a mustache and wore a blue apron, which smelled, though for no obvious reason, of the Auvergne. . . .

"All right, I'll call them. Then I'll have to write my report—and I have to ask you for some details."

"I have nothing more to tell you. Once they find the bomb at the bottom of the Seine . . ."

A man with a blackened face, who, helped by a dog harnessed to the shafts, was trundling a cart along the street below, was giving little toots on a trumpet and yelling at the top of his voice:

"Coal! Get your coal!"

Chave smiled contentedly. The man was on his regular round. This was Belgium. He was in Schaerbeek. Home! . . . After wiping his lips, the inspector rushed away to telephone the news to Paris. Downstairs, no doubt, the old

150

woman was watching, trying to guess what had happened. Foolish old creature, why couldn't she mind her own business? He jumped when he heard a quiet voice in his ear.

"What's wrong, Pierre?"

"Wrong? There's nothing wrong. But I'd like to wash and shave."

"I'll put some water on to boil."

"After that, I must look in at the theater."

"Did you see that young boy who was so sick?"

"Robert, you mean? Yes, I saw Robert."

"What's he doing now?"

"Nothing. I must write to him."

"And the Baron? Don't you think that with his blundering he'll end up by . . ."

She left the phrase unfinished. His eyes were on her, and she thought it wiser to say no more, for the moment, anyhow. Better let time do its work, dulling the edge of his emotions, erasing painful memories. She could guess his present state by the way he was behaving, taking no notice of Pierrot, for instance. He didn't even seem to hear the shrill blasts of the tin trumpet in the next room.

She had placed on the stove a large zinc tub full of water; it served as both washtub and bathtub. After a while he seemed to come out of a dream, and he asked her in an almost casual voice:

"Got enough money?"

"Well, I paid the gas bill yesterday, and I have only thirty francs left."

He listened with half an ear; his thoughts were wandering again. He'd have to get back to the old life gradually, not rush matters. After another pause, he asked:

"What day is it today?"

"Friday."

"Do you think Pierrot can go out?"

"Tomorrow, perhaps, or the day after."

He was squatting in the tub, which stood on a square of linoleum they always put on the bedroom floor for baths. Squeezing a soapy sponge against his shoulder, he shouted to the kitchen:

"Let's say Sunday, then. How about going for a picnic by the river if the weather's good? . . . Hand me a towel, will you?"

She ran in with it and hurried out again, to make sure the beans weren't burning. They went on talking from one room to the other, missing a remark now and then because of the noise of the tin trumpet and sounds of splashing, saucepans being moved, a fire being poked.

"I'll go to the theater this afternoon. I don't imagine they'll have found anyone to replace me."

And so on, gently, cautiously, since they had the feeling that all this was fragile, and they didn't want to break anything. . . .